Best Buddies
Save the Duck!

Written by
Vicky Fang

Art by
Luisa Leal

SCHOLASTIC INC.

To my editor, Katie. — VF
To my Mom, Maria Lourdes. — LL

Text copyright © 2023 by Vicky Fang
Illustrations copyright © 2023 by Luisa Leal

All rights reserved. Published by Scholastic Inc., *Publishers since 1920.* SCHOLASTIC, ACORN, and associated logos are trademarks and/or registered trademarks of Scholastic Inc.

The publisher does not have any control over and does not assume any responsibility for author or third-party websites or their content.

No part of this publication may be reproduced, stored in a retrieval system, or transmitted in any form or by any means, electronic, mechanical, photocopying, recording, or otherwise, without written permission of the publisher. For information regarding permission, write to Scholastic Inc., Attention: Permissions Department, 557 Broadway, New York, NY 10012.

This book is a work of fiction. Names, characters, places, and incidents are either the product of the author's imagination or are used fictitiously, and any resemblance to actual persons, living or dead, business establishments, events, or locales is entirely coincidental.

Library of Congress Cataloging-in-Publication Data

Names: Fang, Vicky, author. | Leal, Luisa, illustrator.
Title: Save the duck! / written by Vicky Fang ; illustrated by Luisa Leal.
Description: First edition. | New York : Acorn/Scholastic, Inc., 2023. | Series: Best Buddies; 2 | Audience: Ages 4–6. | Audience: Grades K–1. |
Summary: Across three humorous short stories, Sniff and Scratch have fun with toilet paper, chasing each other's tails, and snuggling with Sniff's stuffed duck.
Identifiers: LCCN 2022043676 (print) | ISBN 9781338865608 (paperback) |
ISBN 9781338865615 (library binding)
Subjects: CYAC: Dogs—Fiction. | Cats—Fiction. | Best friends—Fiction. |
Friendship—Fiction. | Humorous stories. | LCGFT: Humorous fiction. | Picture books.
Classification: LCC PZ7.1.F3543 Sav 2023 (print) | DDC [E]—dc23
LC record available at https://lccn.loc.gov/2022043676

10 9 8 7 6 5 4 3 2 1   23 24 25 26 27

Printed in India   197

First edition, December 2023
Edited by Katie Carella
Book design by Maria Mercado

The Roll

This is Sniff.

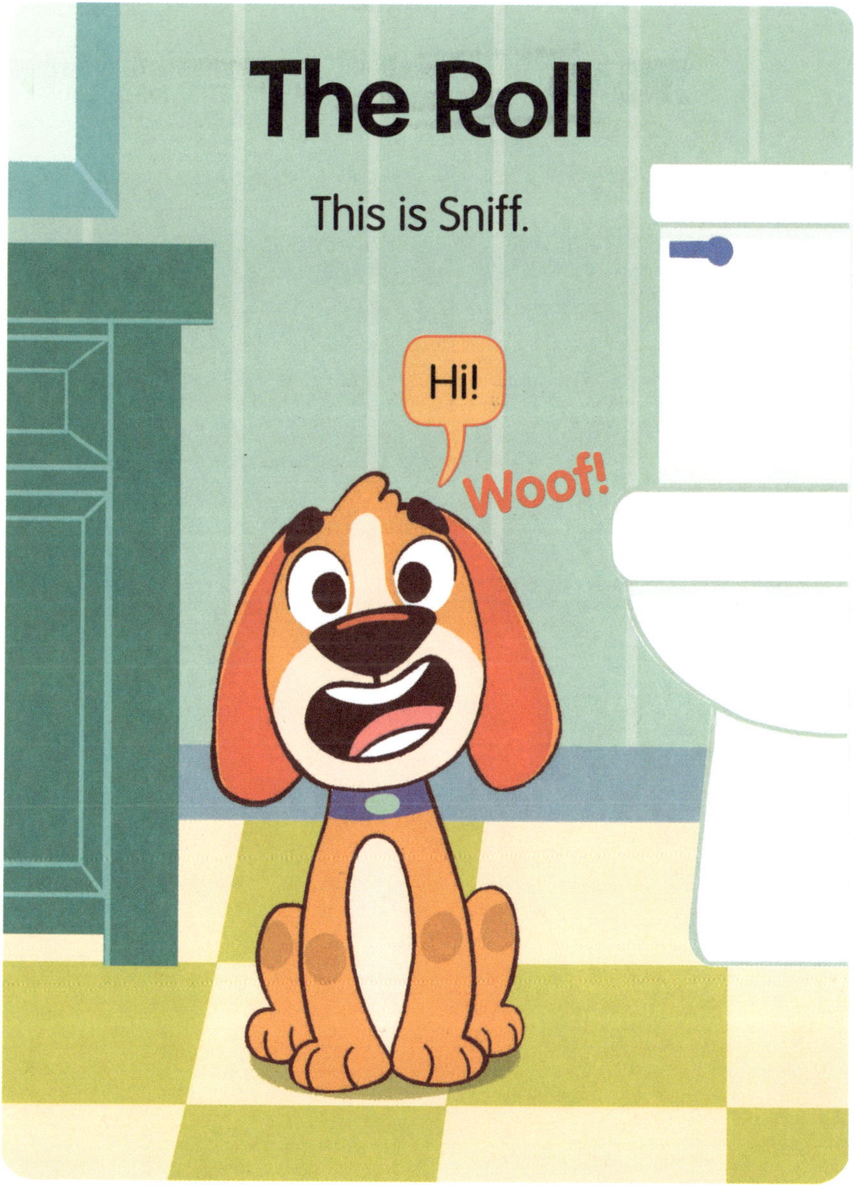
Hi!
Woof!

This is Scratch.

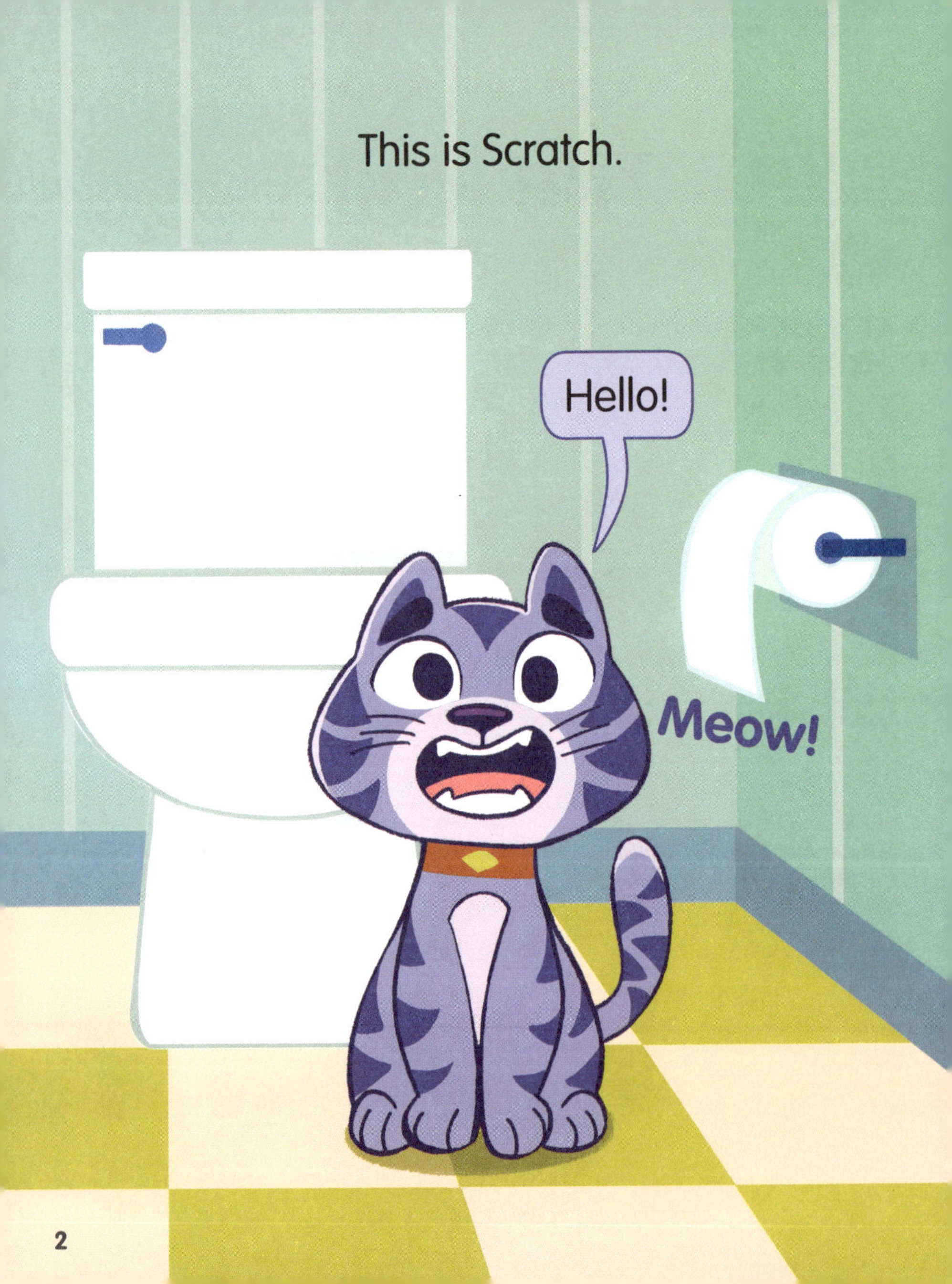
Hello!
Meow!

They are best buddies.

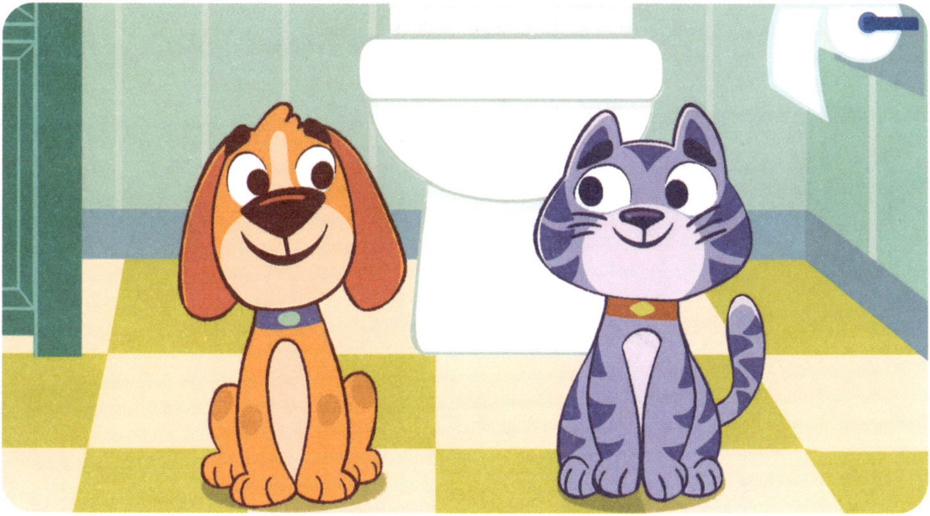

Well, sometimes.

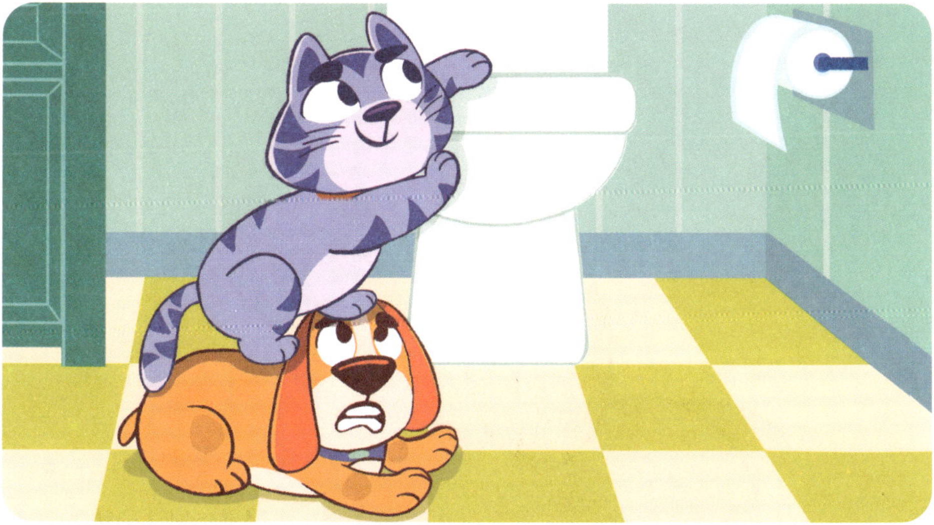

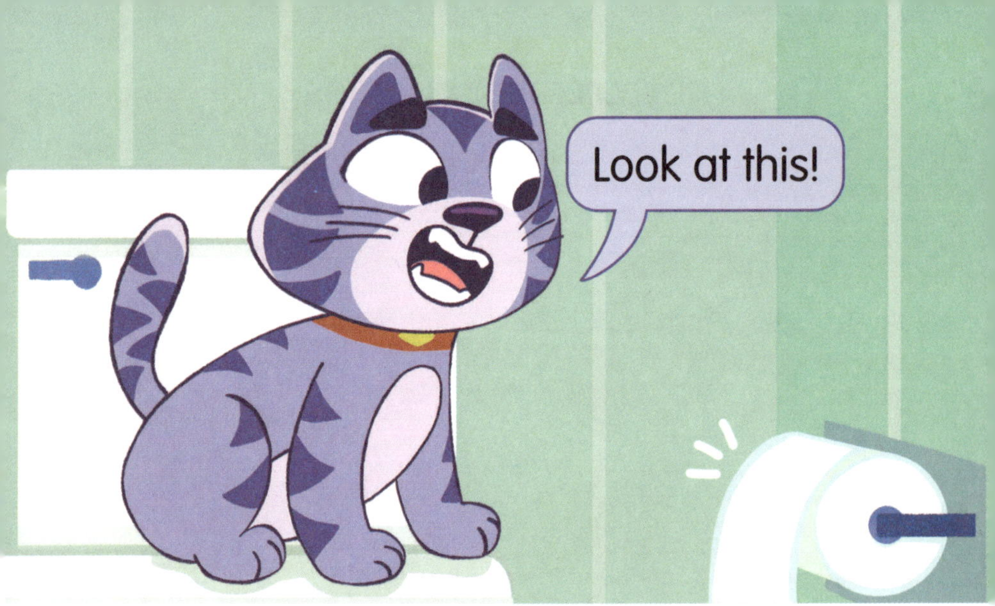
Look at this!

Sniff sniffs.

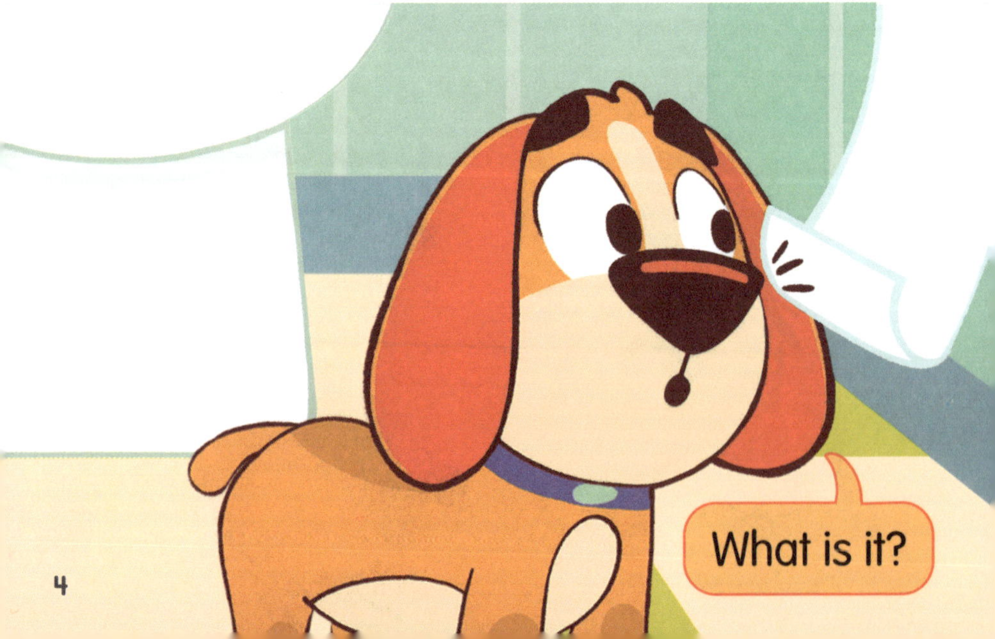
What is it?

Scratch scratches.

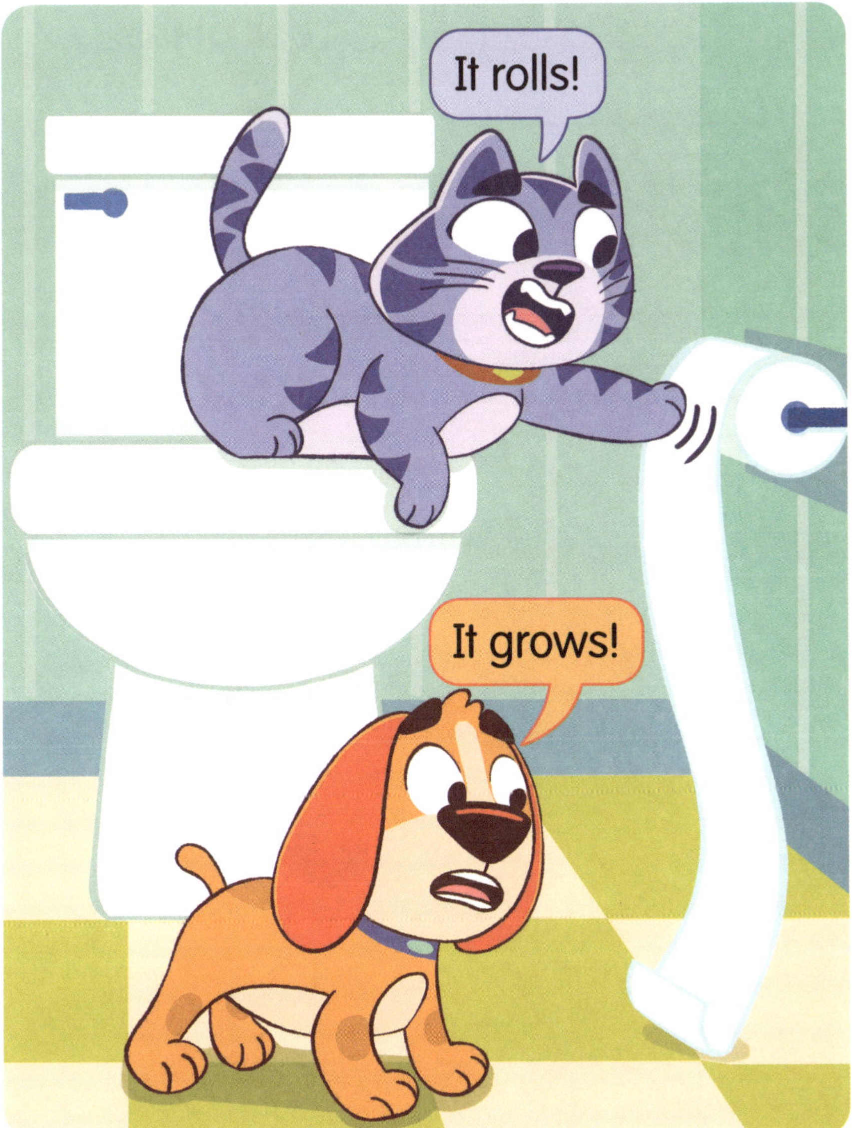
It rolls!
It grows!

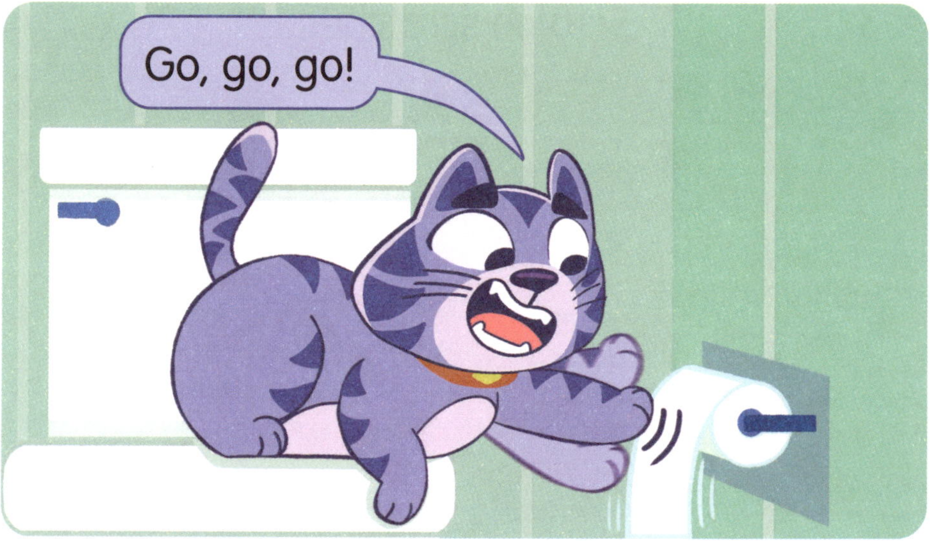
Go, go, go!

So Sniff goes.

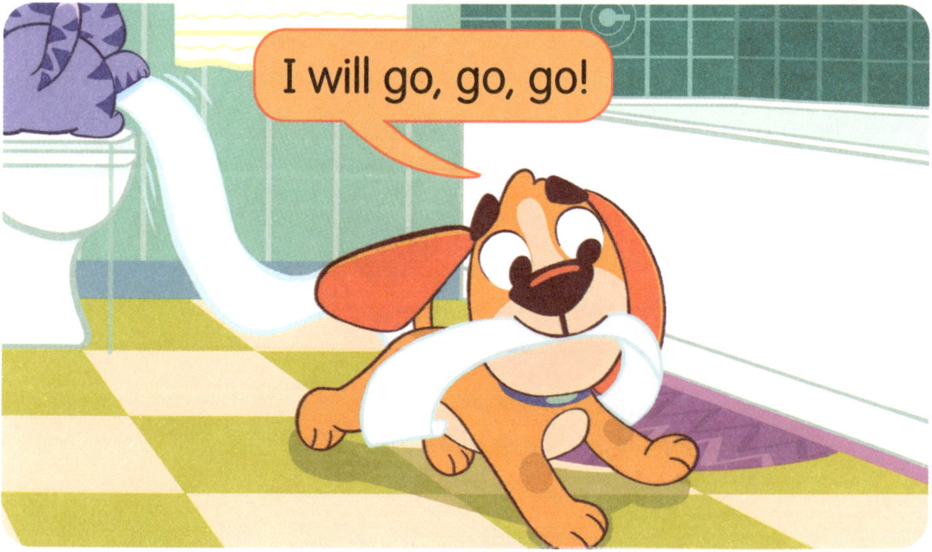
I will go, go, go!

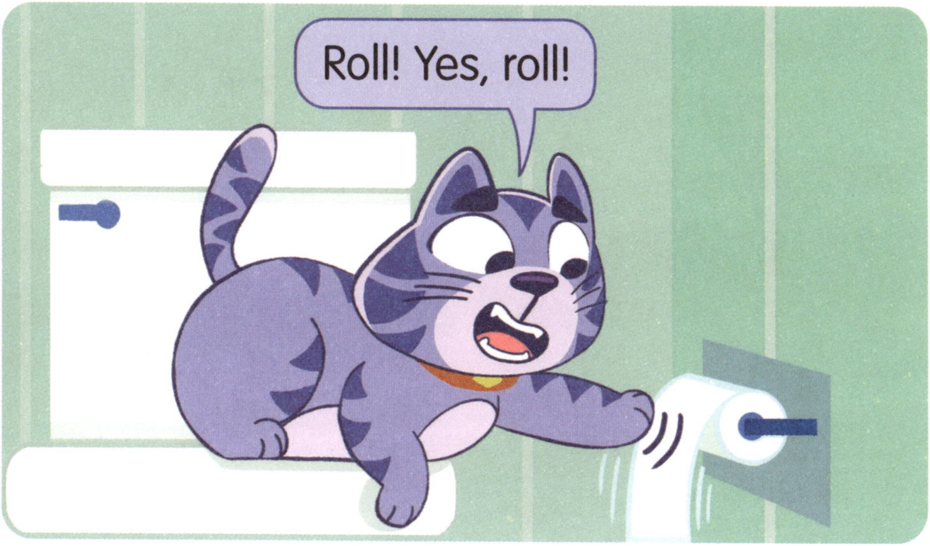
Roll! Yes, roll!

So Sniff rolls.

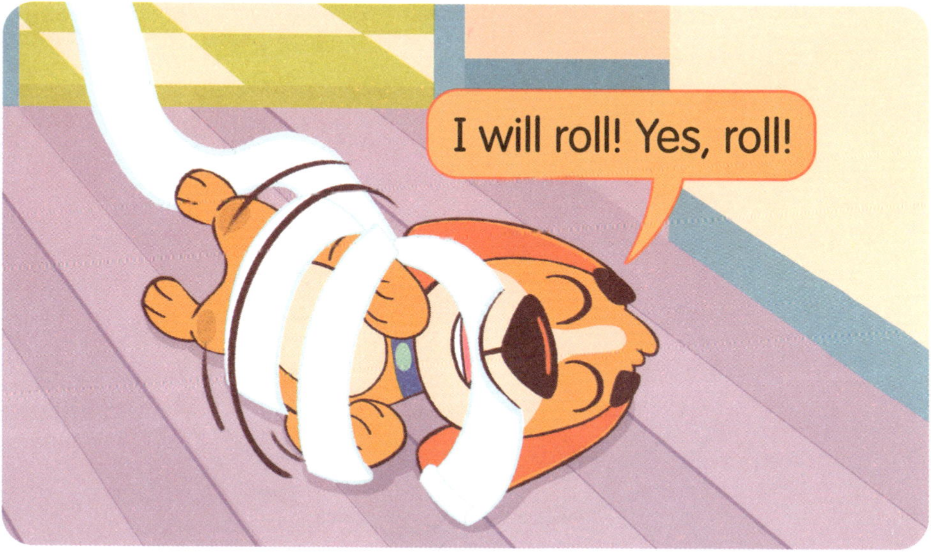
I will roll! Yes, roll!

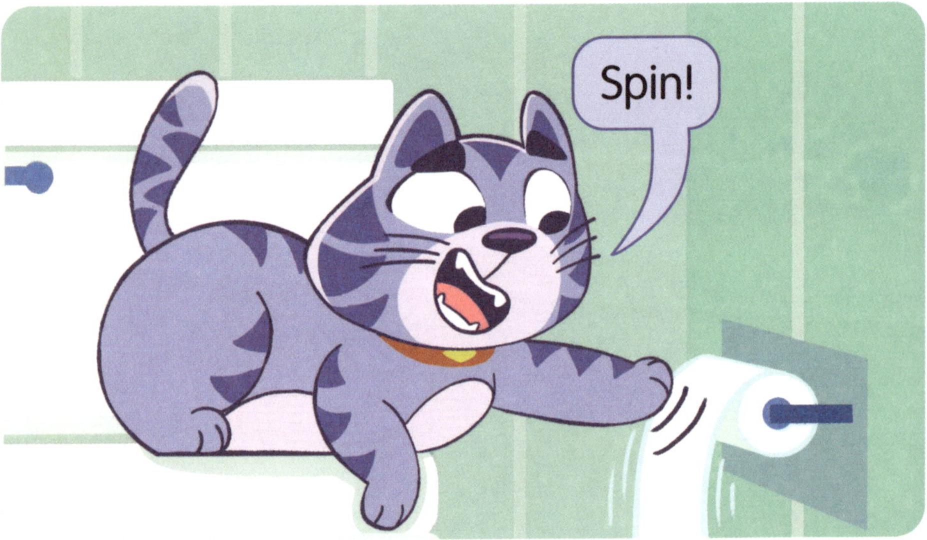
Spin!

So Sniff spins.

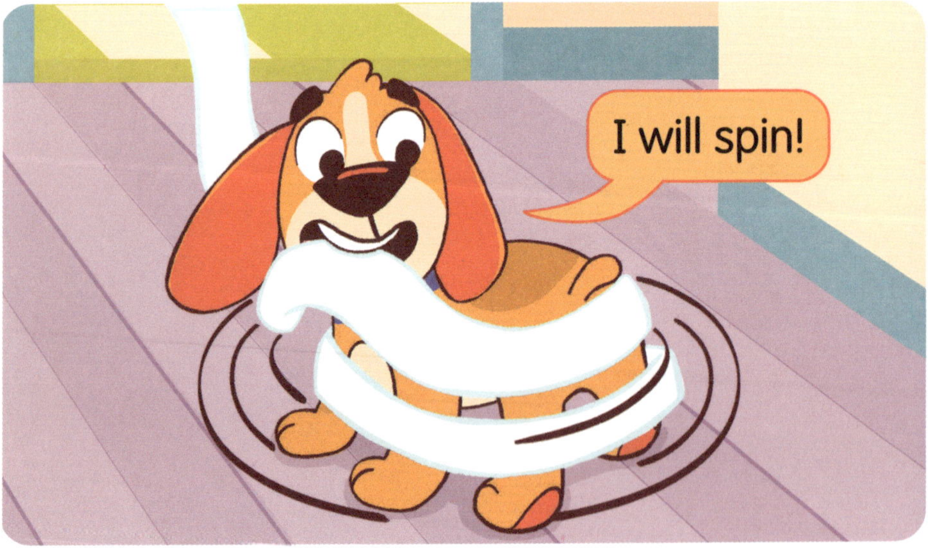
I will spin!

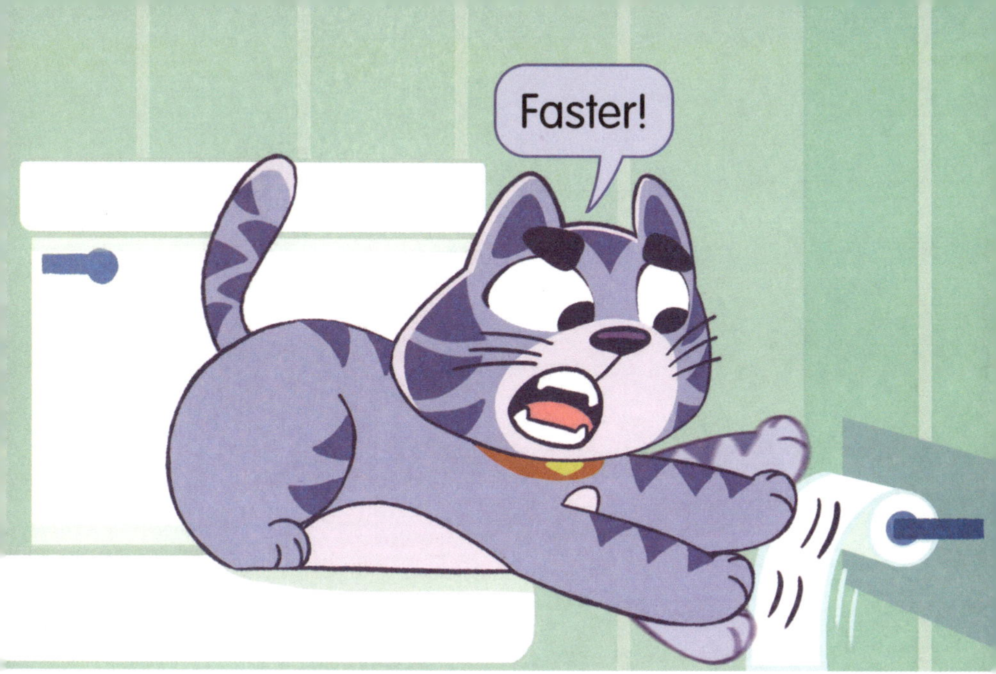
Faster!

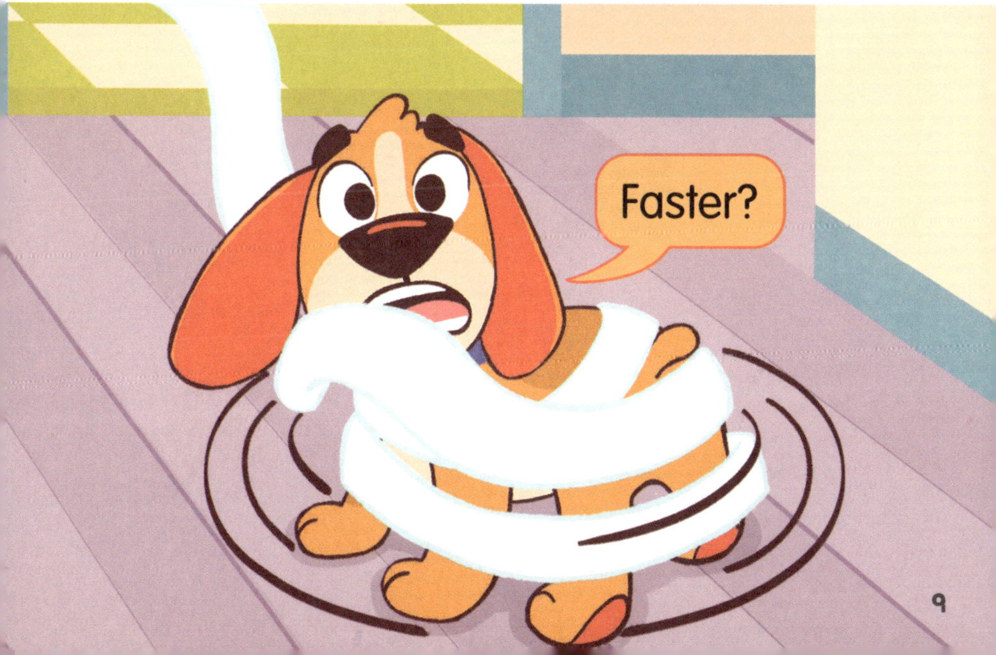
Faster?

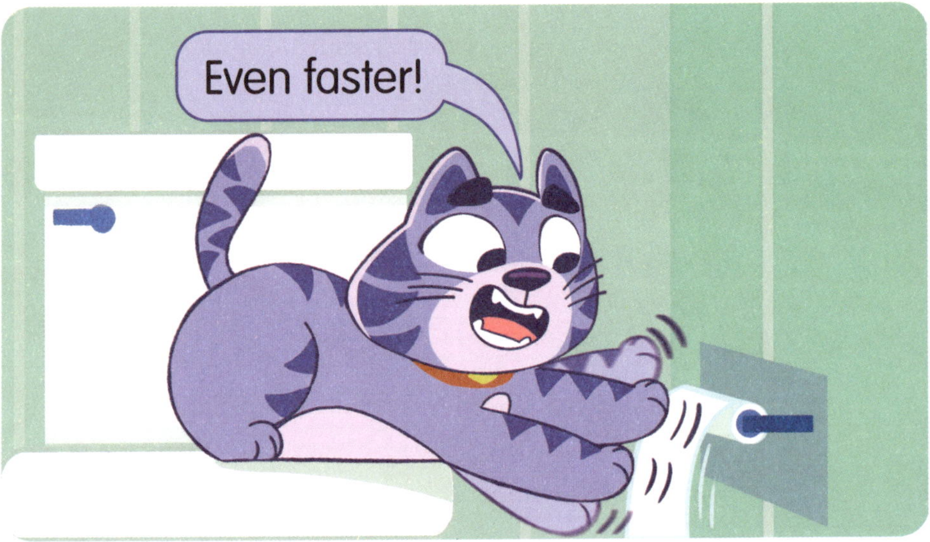
Even faster!

Sniff spins faster.

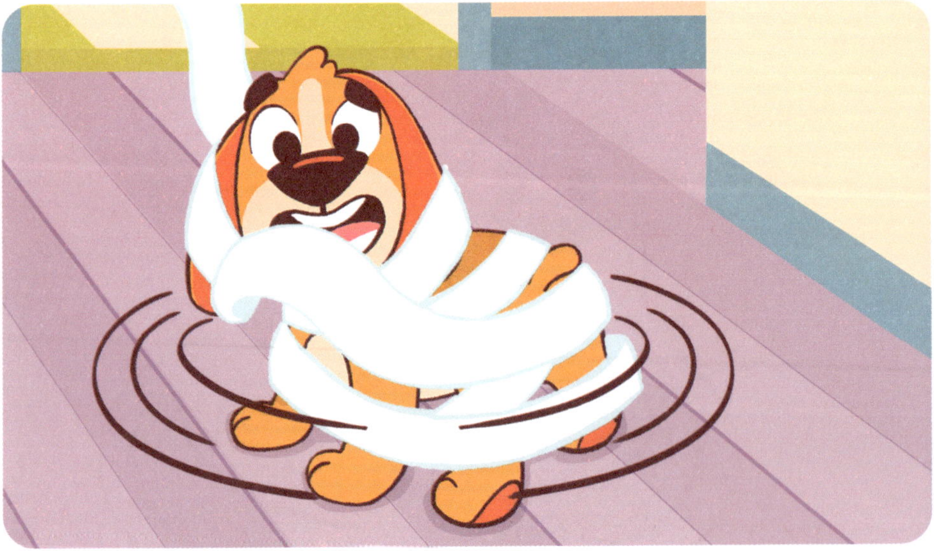

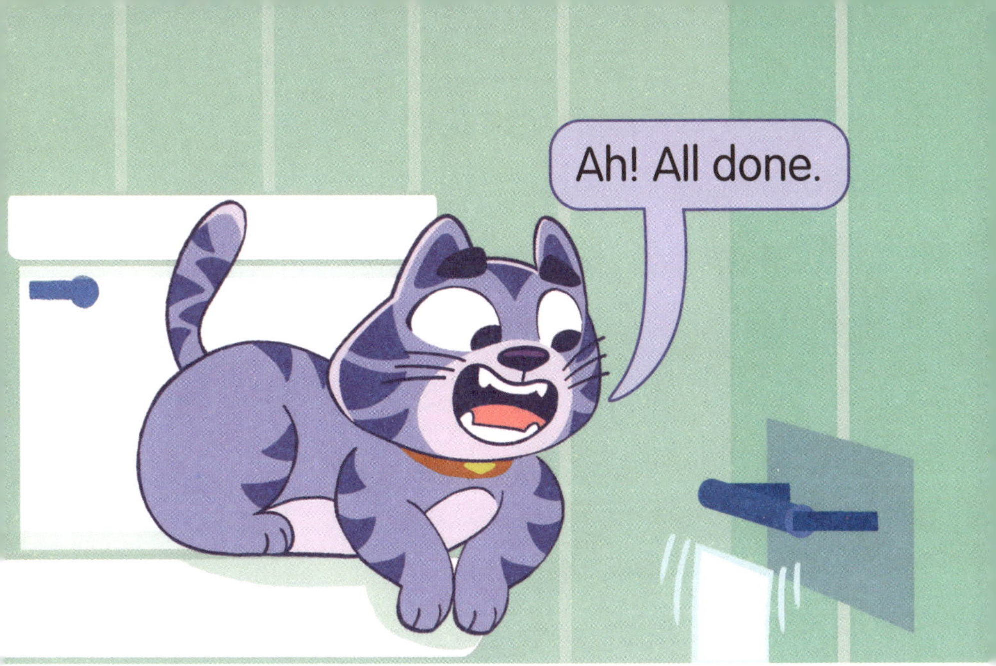
Ah! All done.

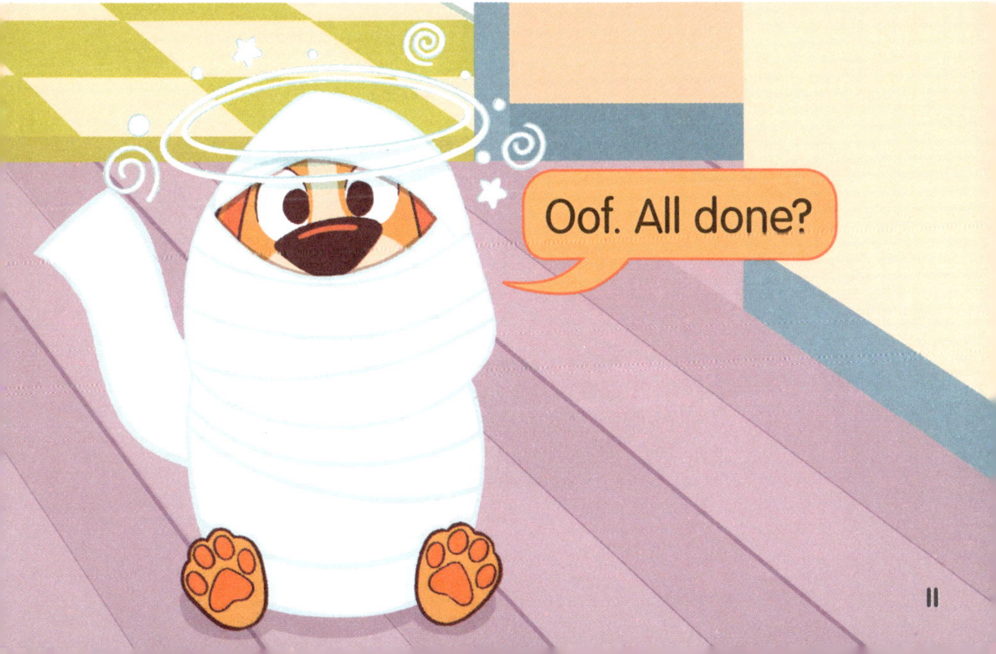
Oof. All done?

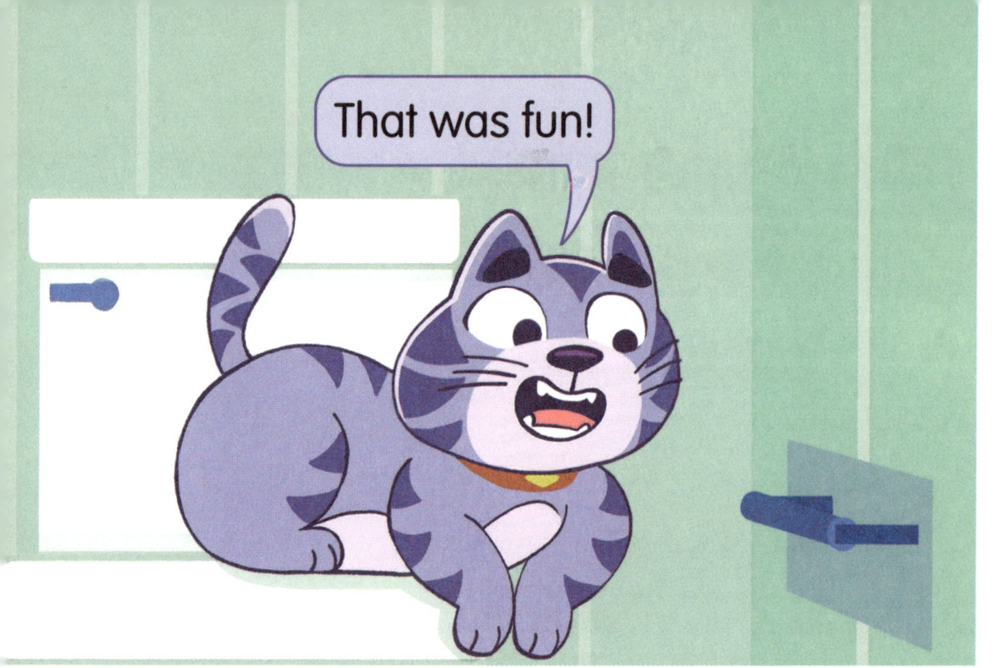
That was fun!

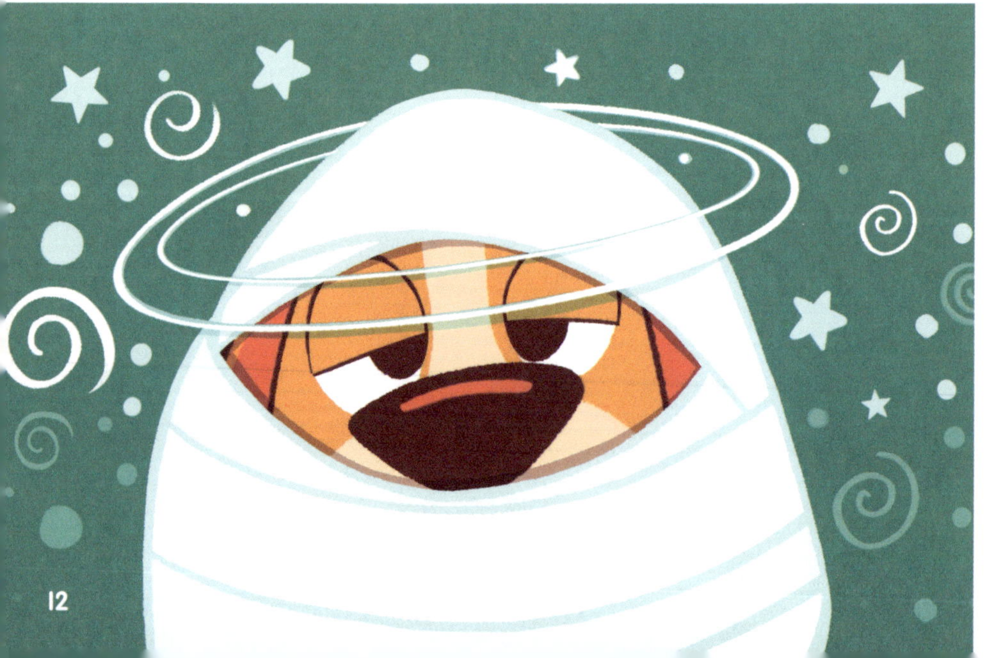

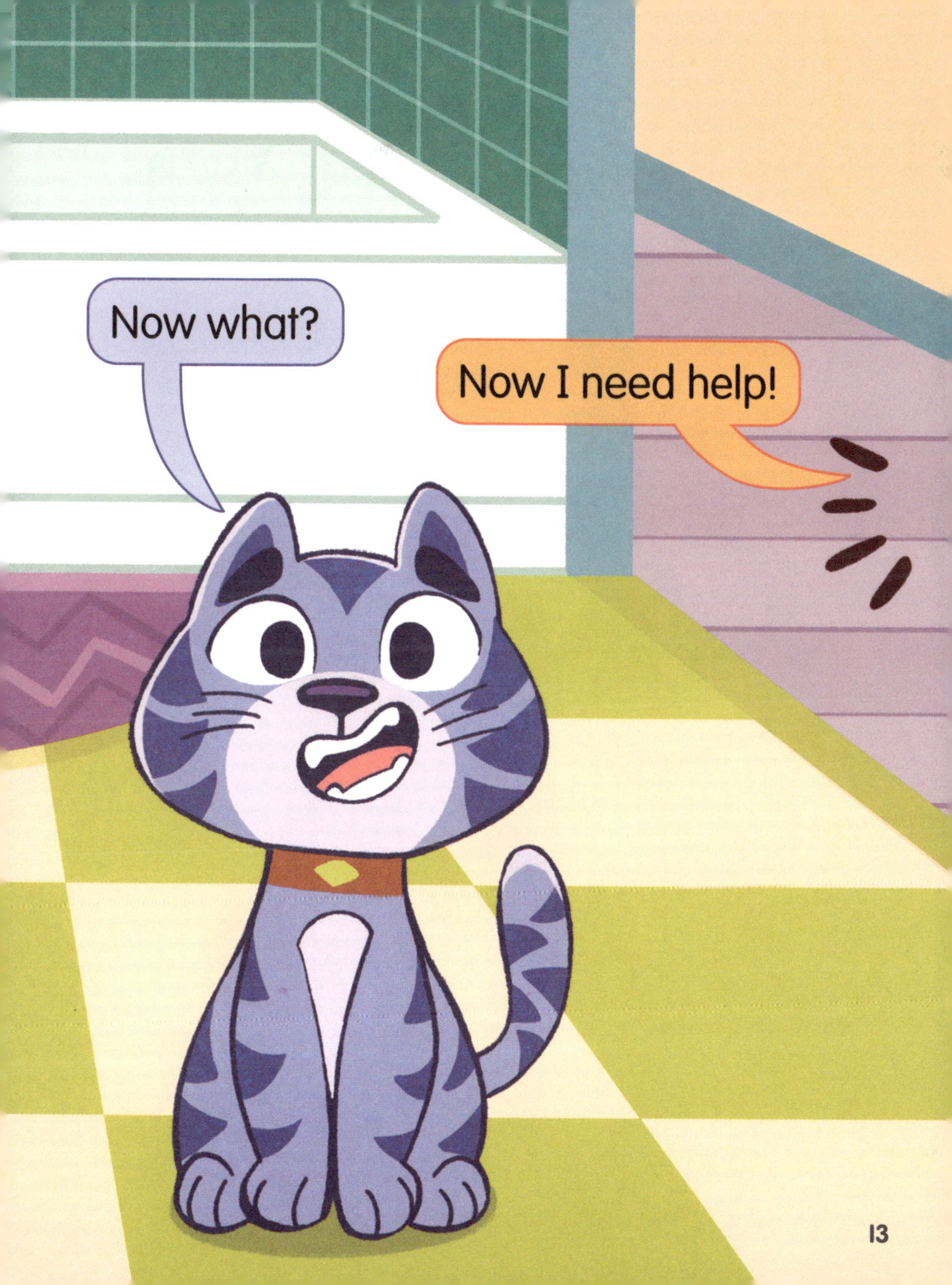
Now what?
Now I need help!

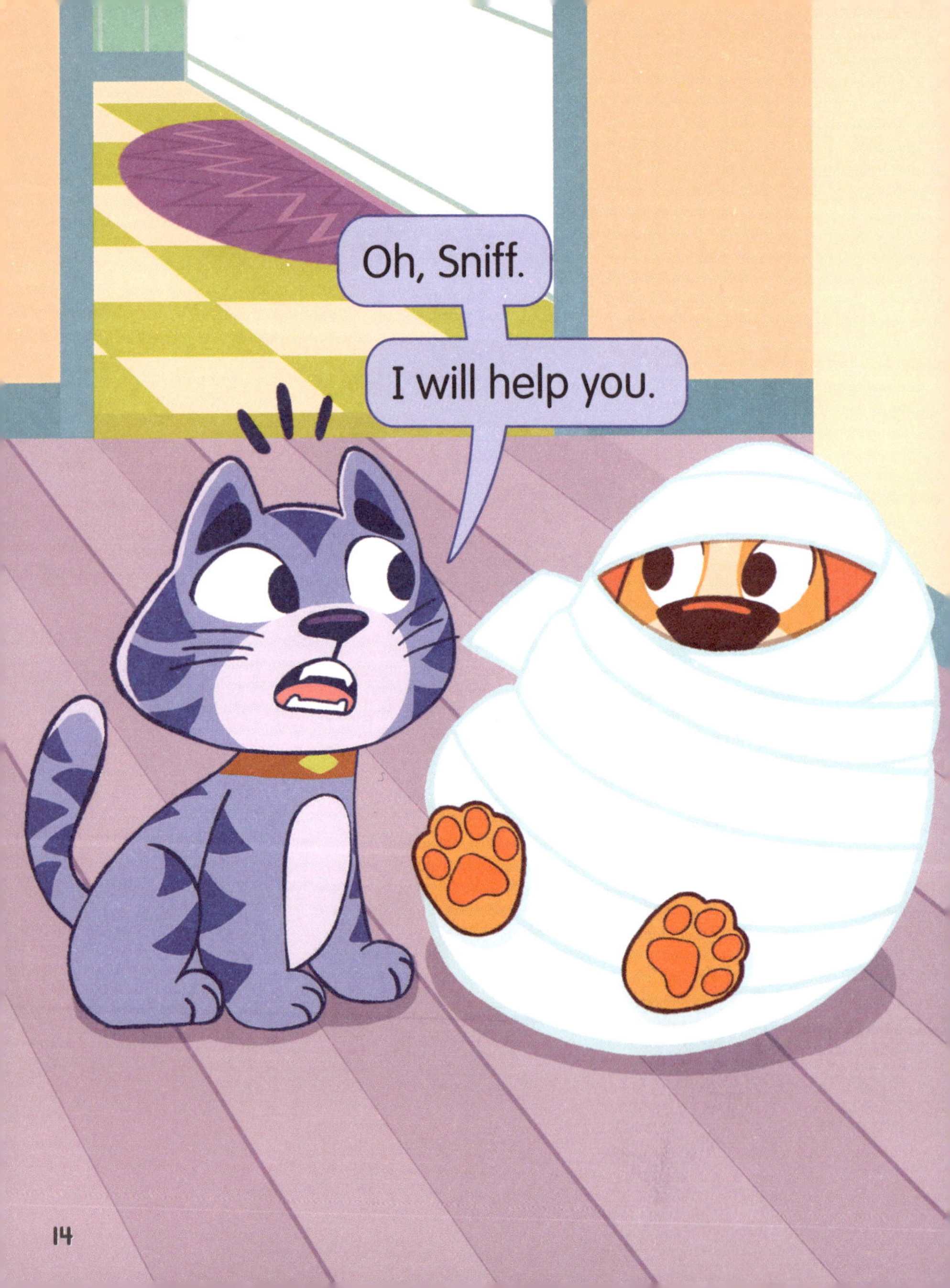
Oh, Sniff.
I will help you.

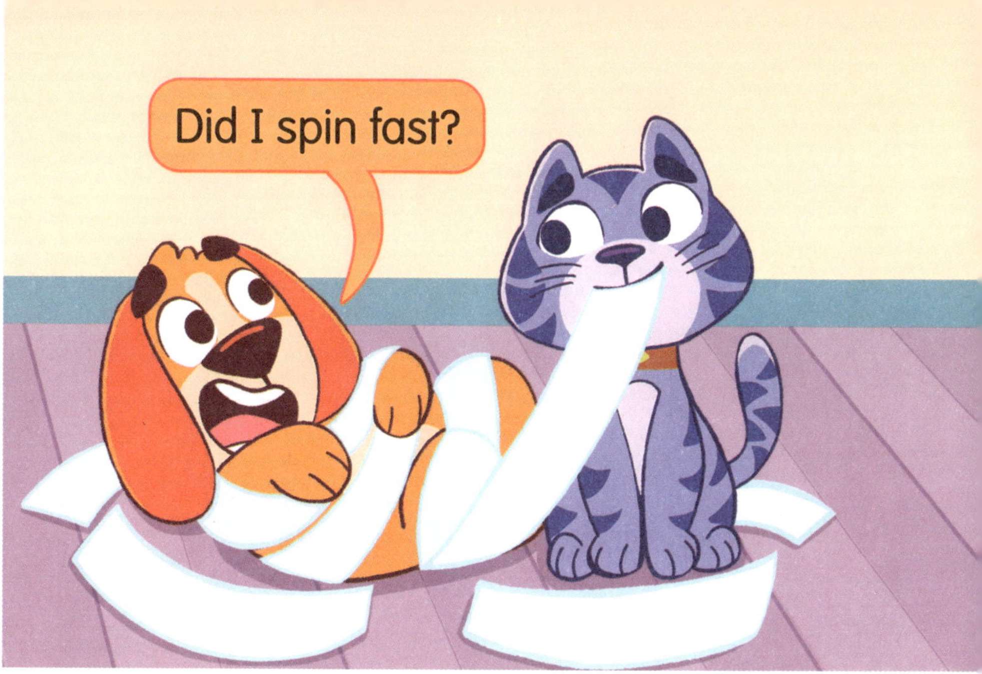
Did I spin fast?

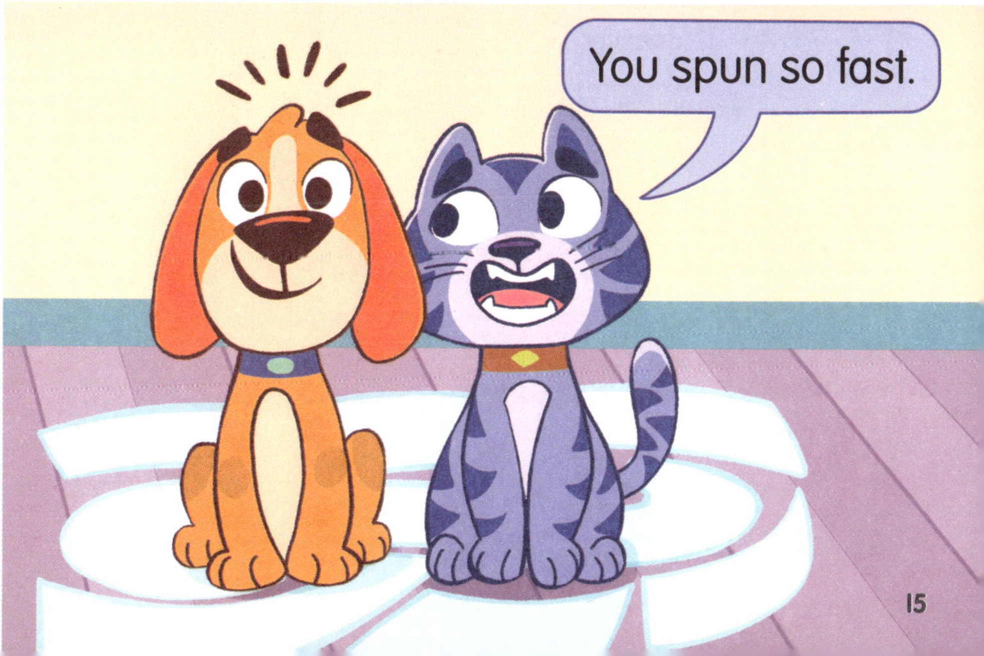
You spun so fast.

The Tail

A tail moves.

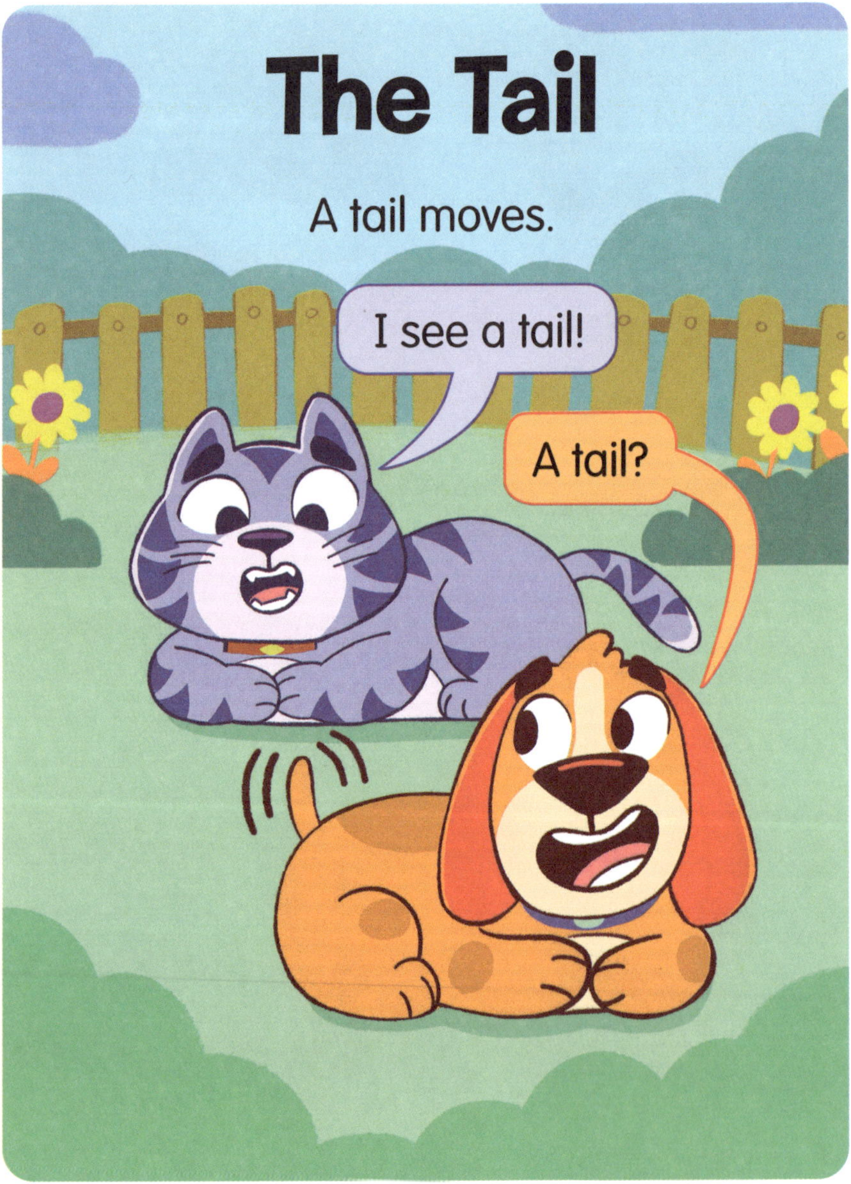
I see a tail!
A tail?

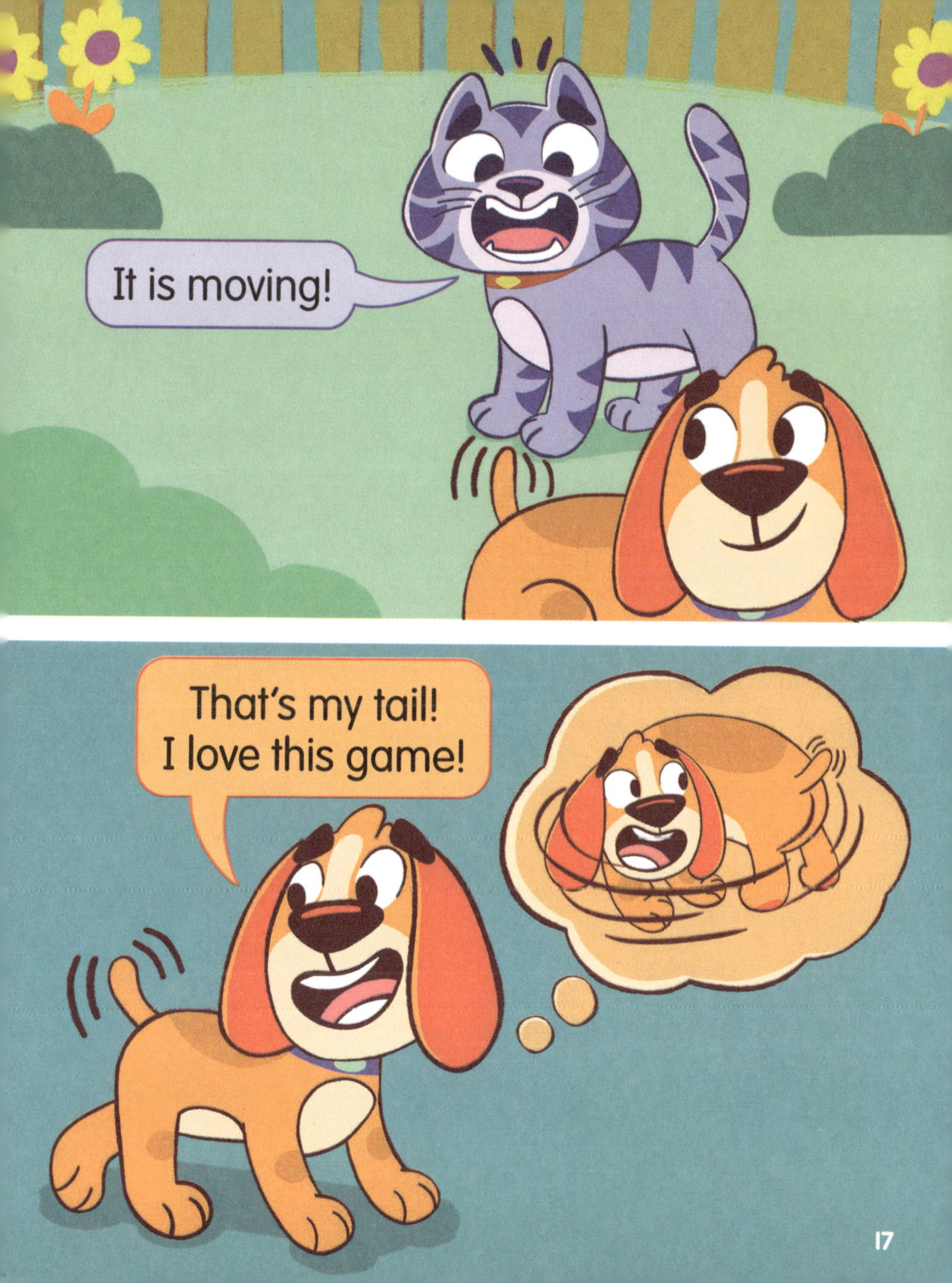
It is moving!
That's my tail!
I love this game!

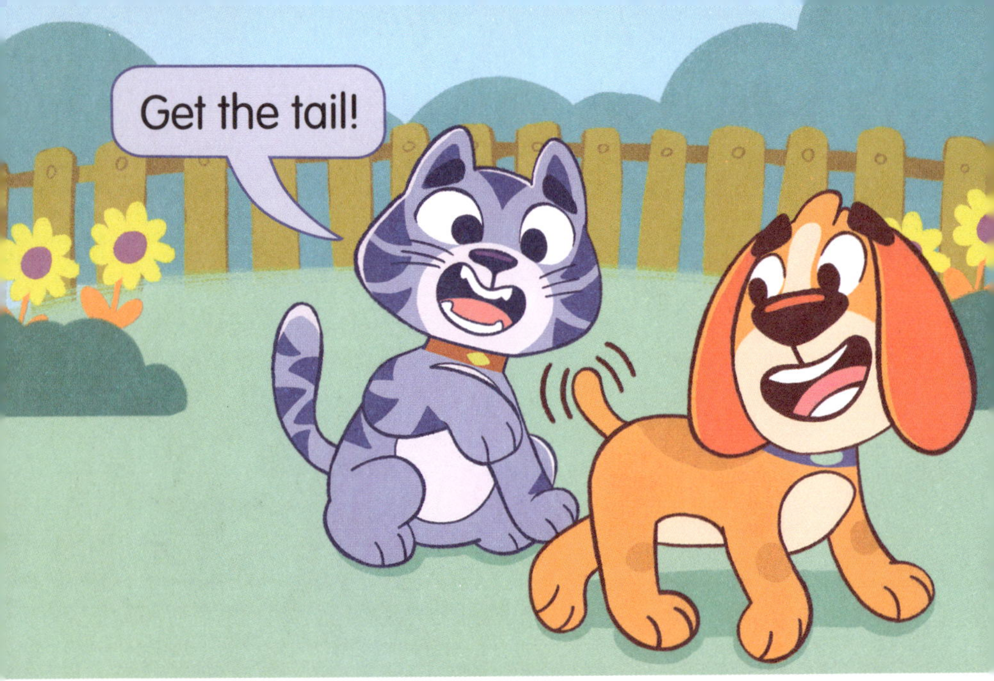
Get the tail!

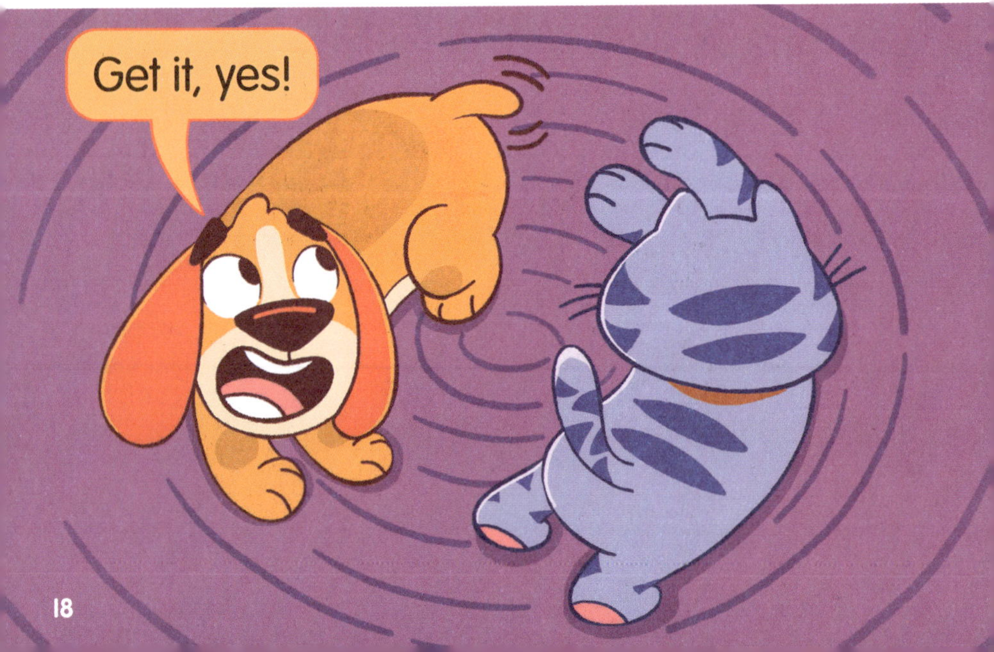
Get it, yes!

Sniff and Scratch chase the tail.

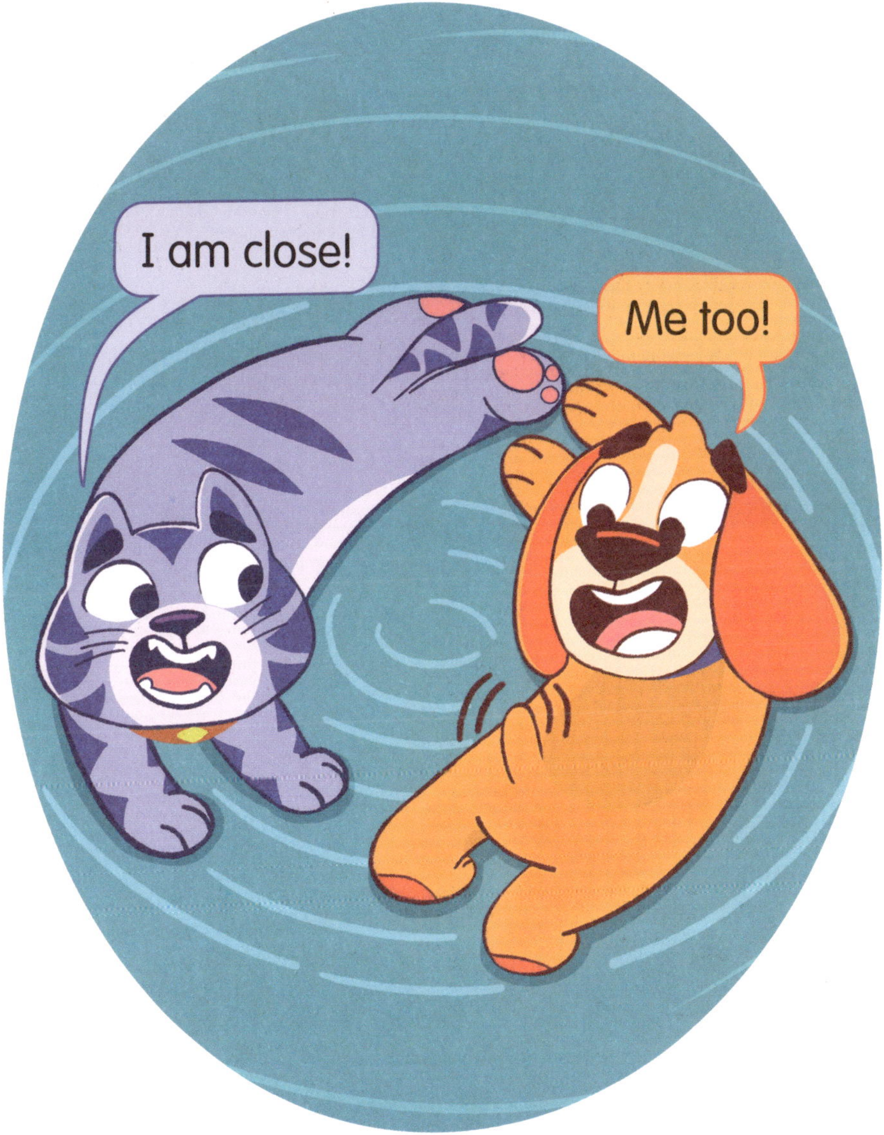
I am close!
Me too!

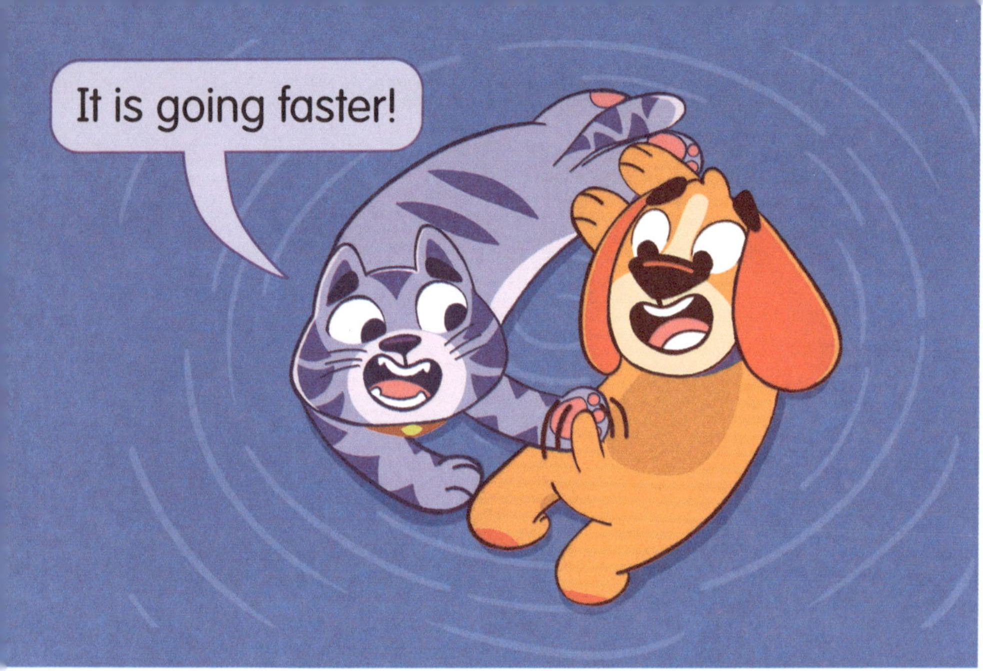
It is going faster!

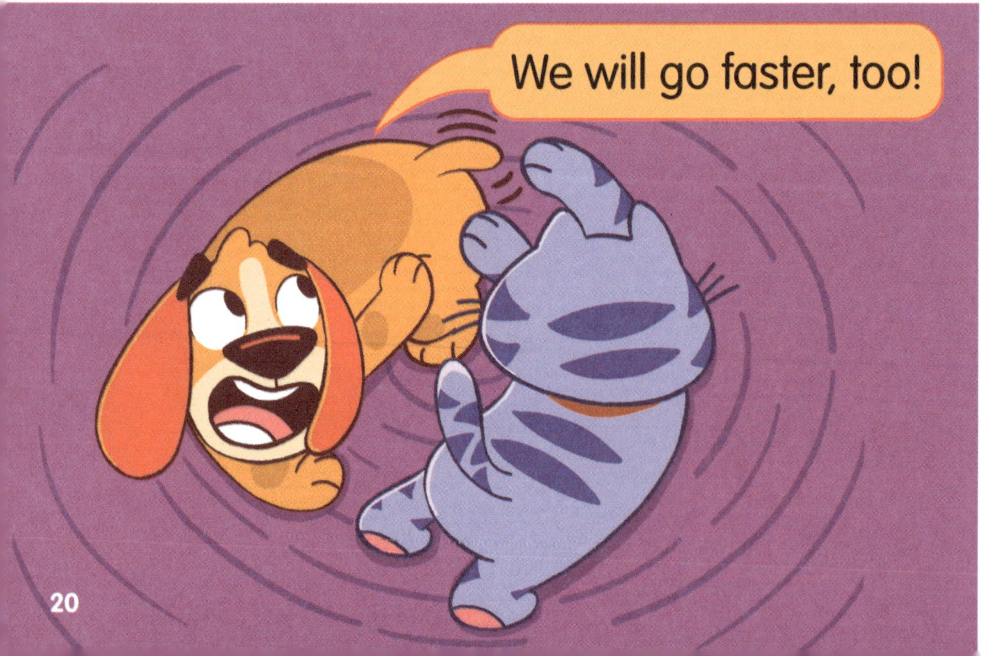
We will go faster, too!

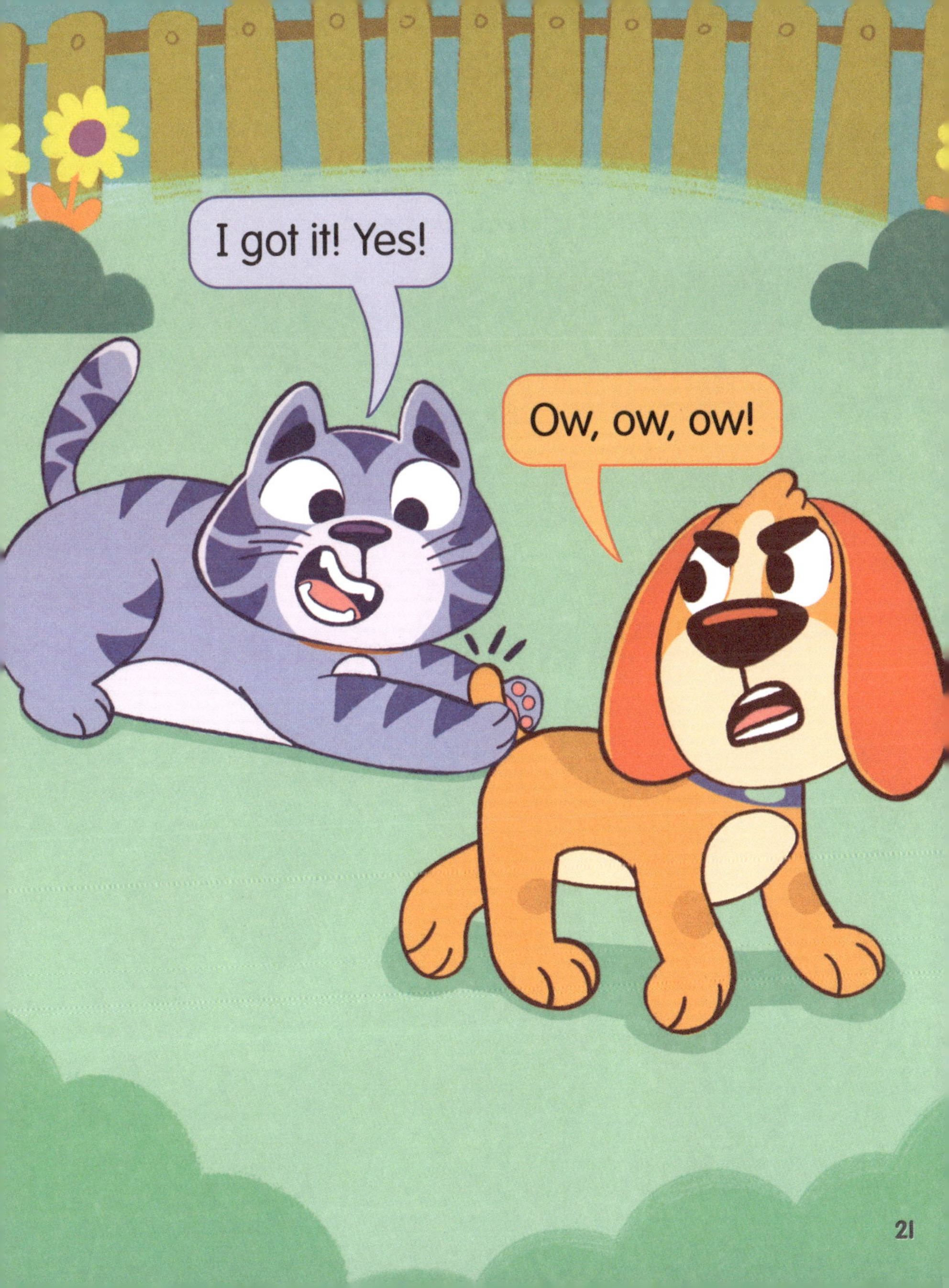
I got it! Yes!
Ow, ow, ow!

Scratch is happy.

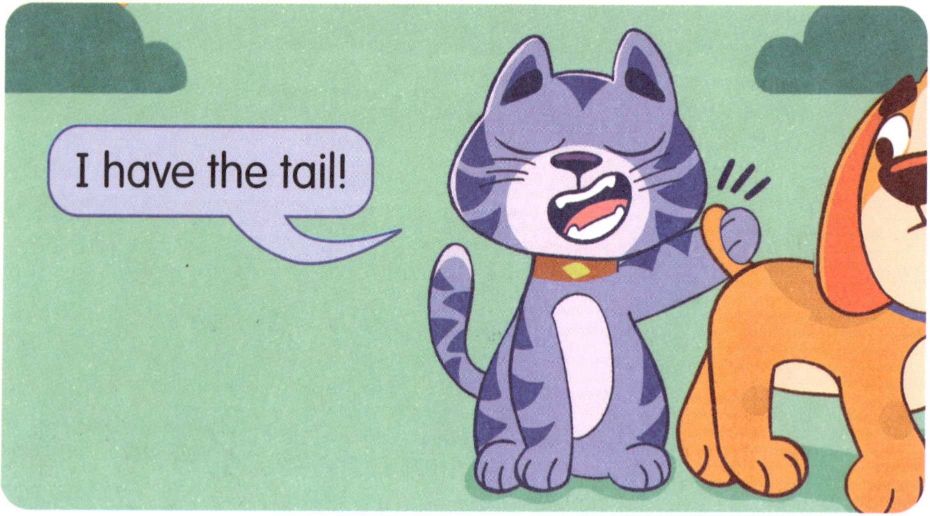
I have the tail!

Sniff is not happy.

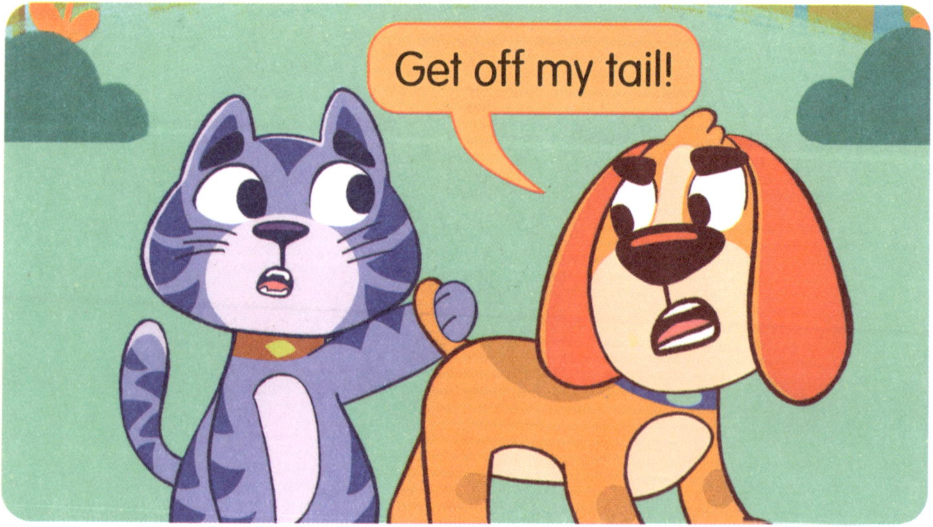
Get off my tail!

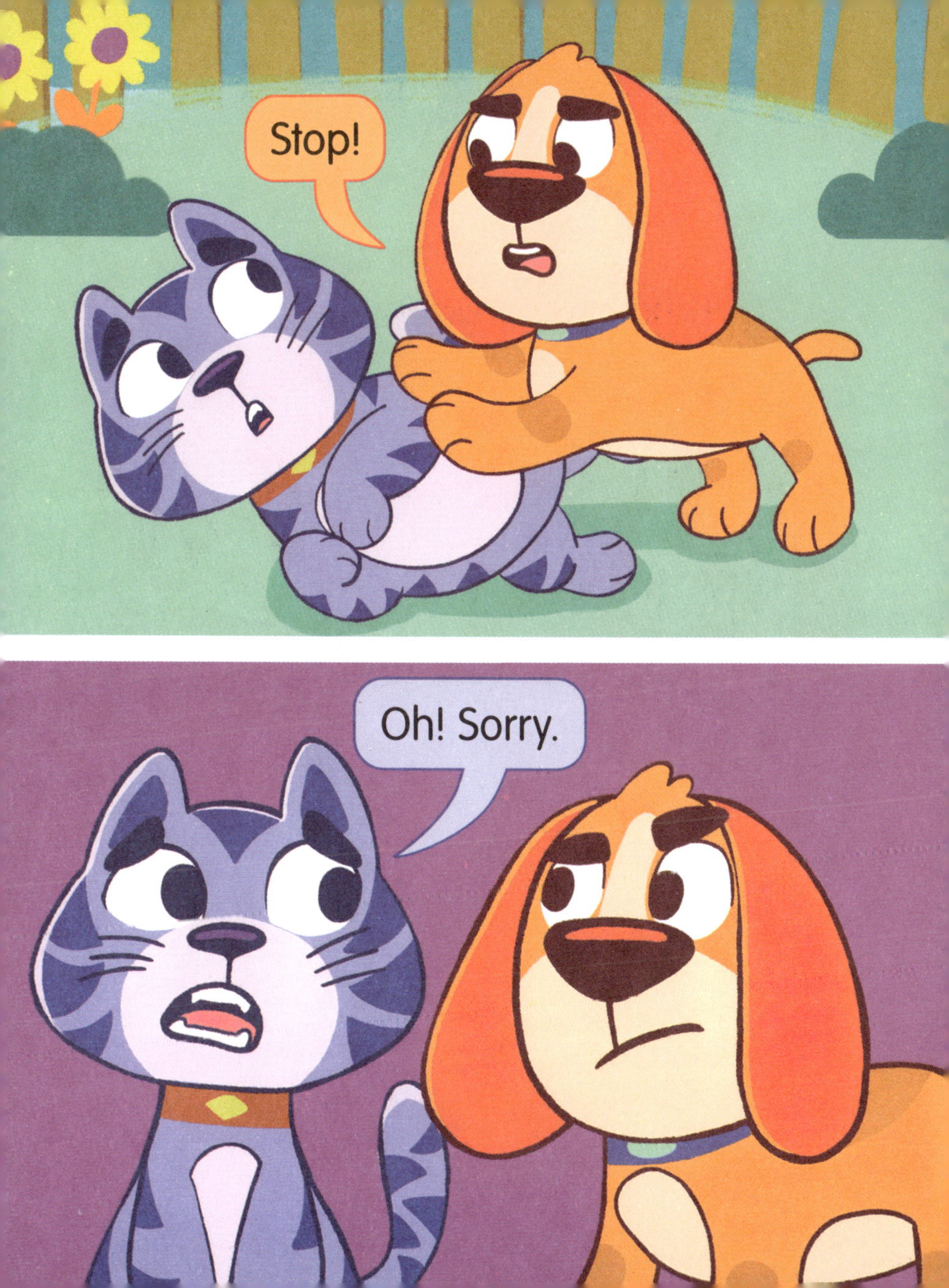
Stop!
Oh! Sorry.

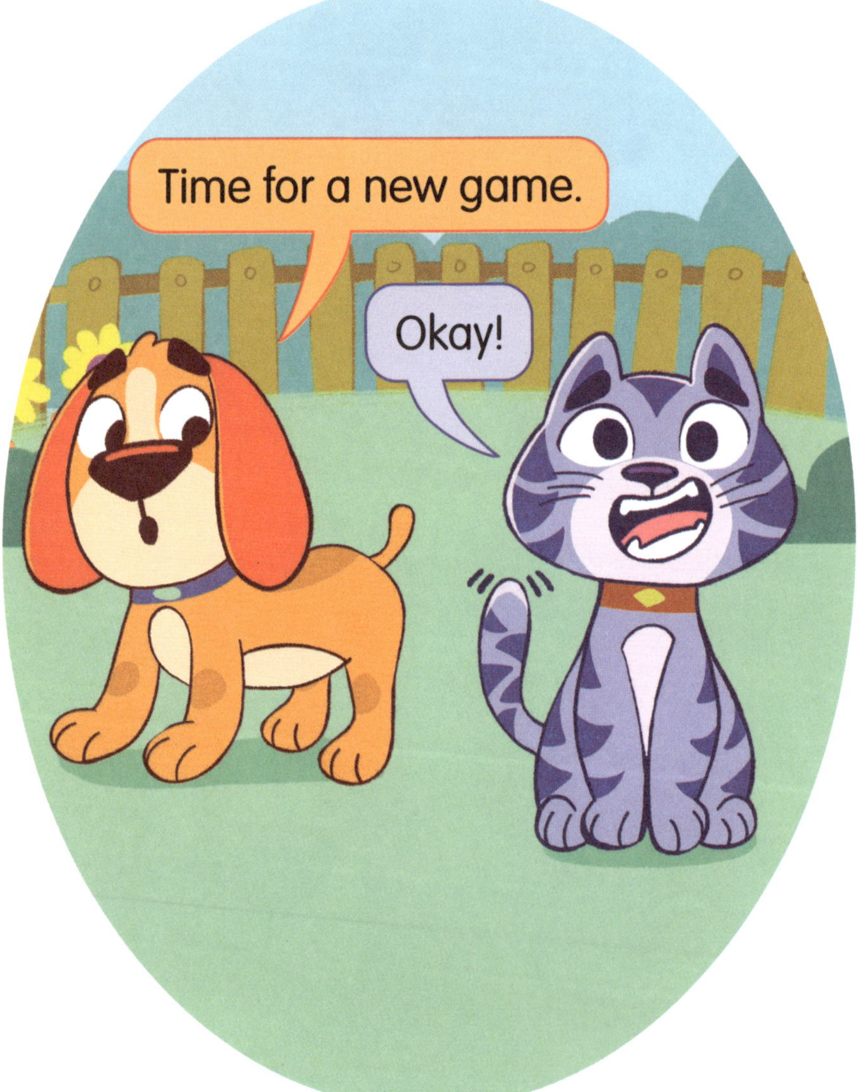
Time for a new game.
Okay!

A tail moves.

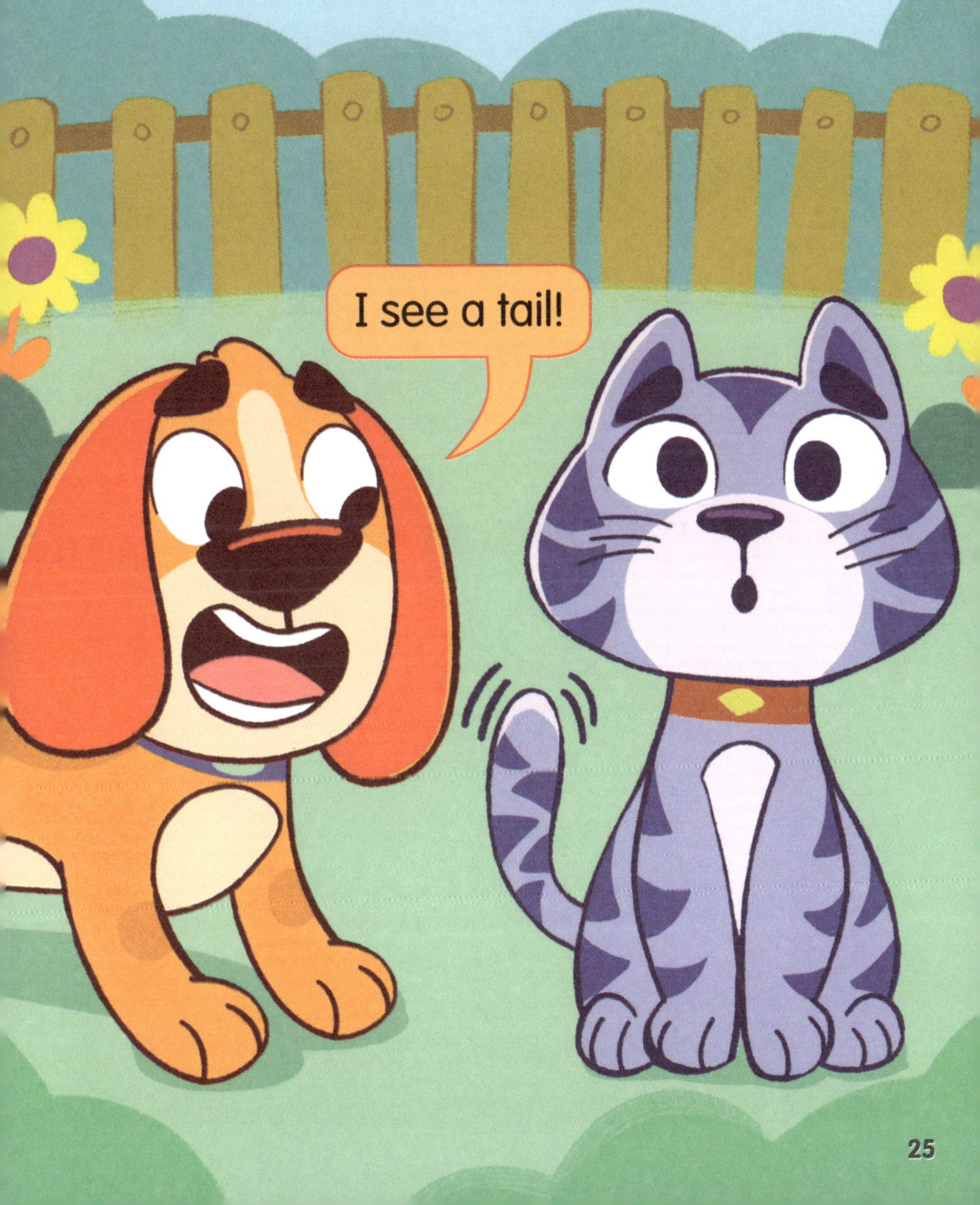
I see a tail!

The Toy

There is a duck.

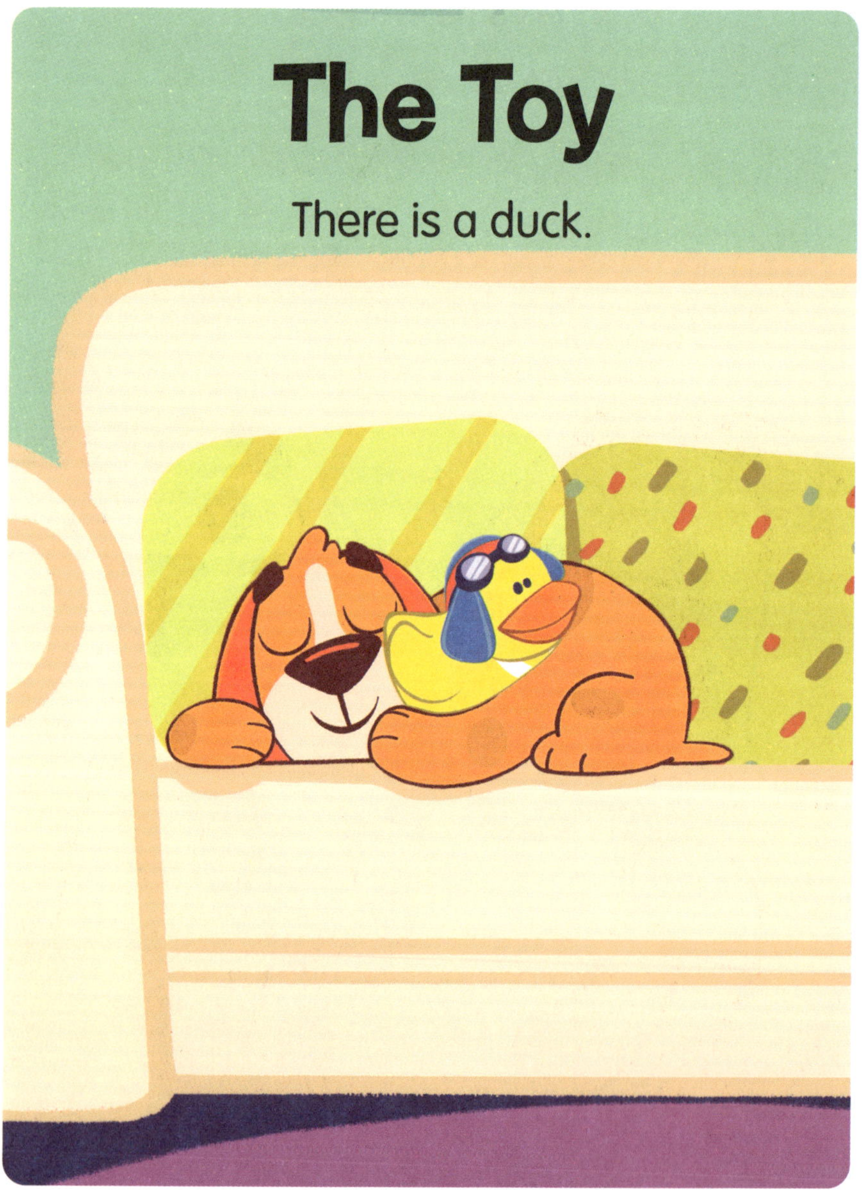

Scratch sees the duck.

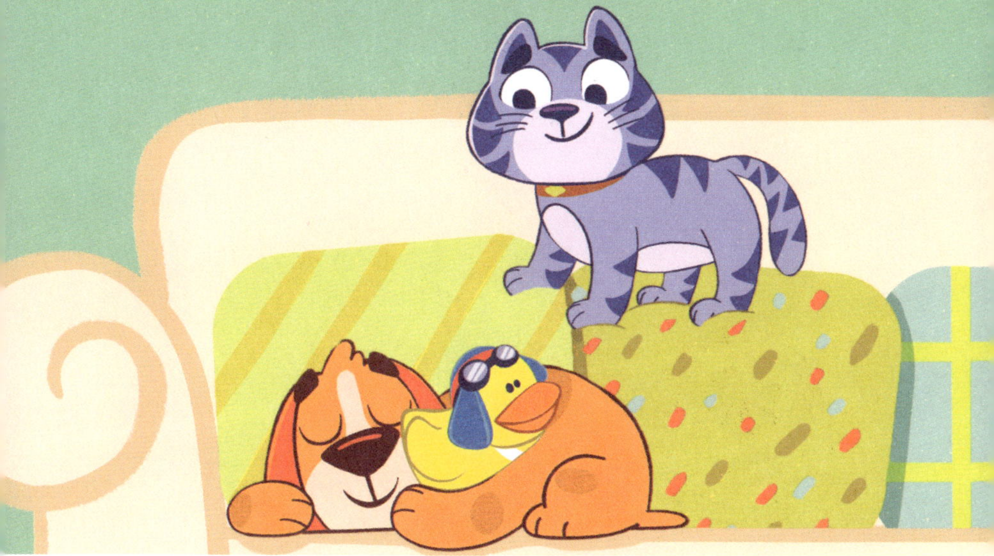

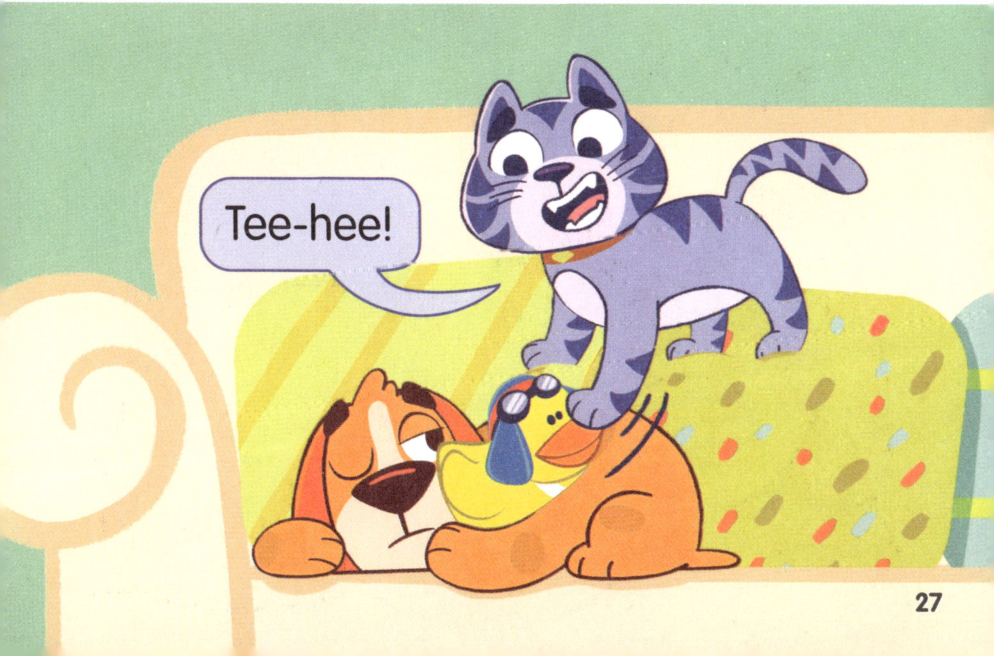
Tee-hee!

Scratch takes the duck.

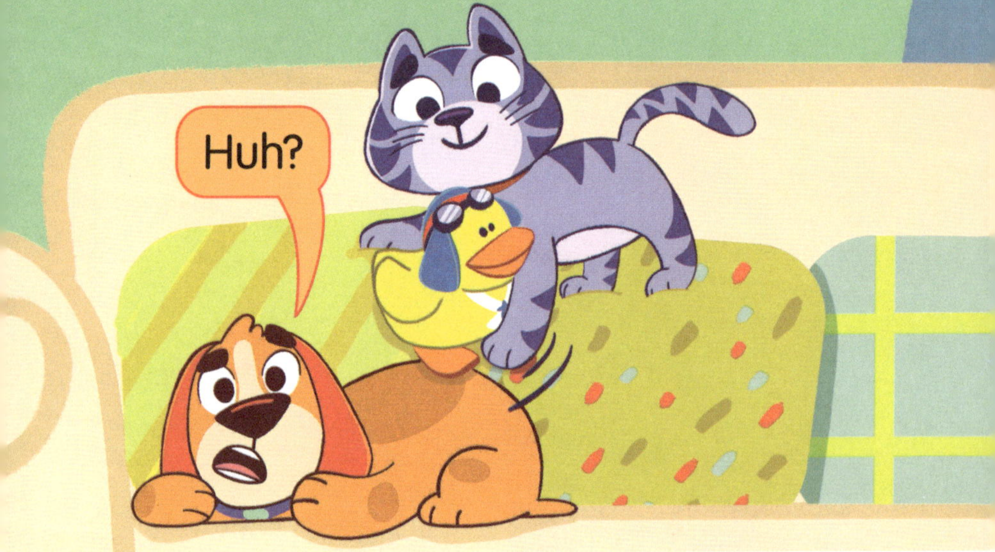
Huh?

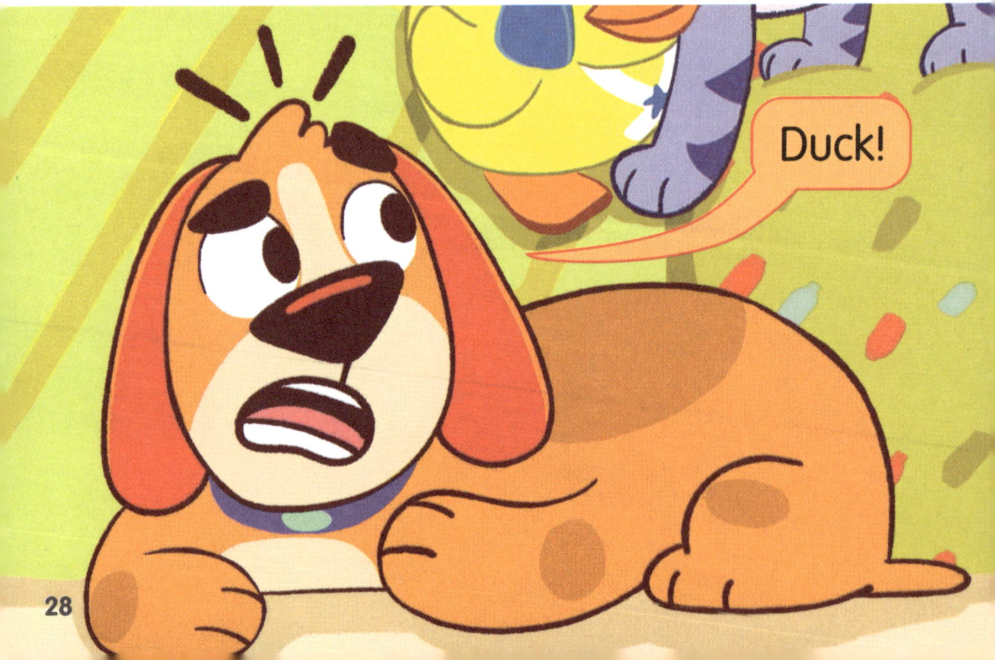
Duck!

Sniff and Scratch tug at the duck.

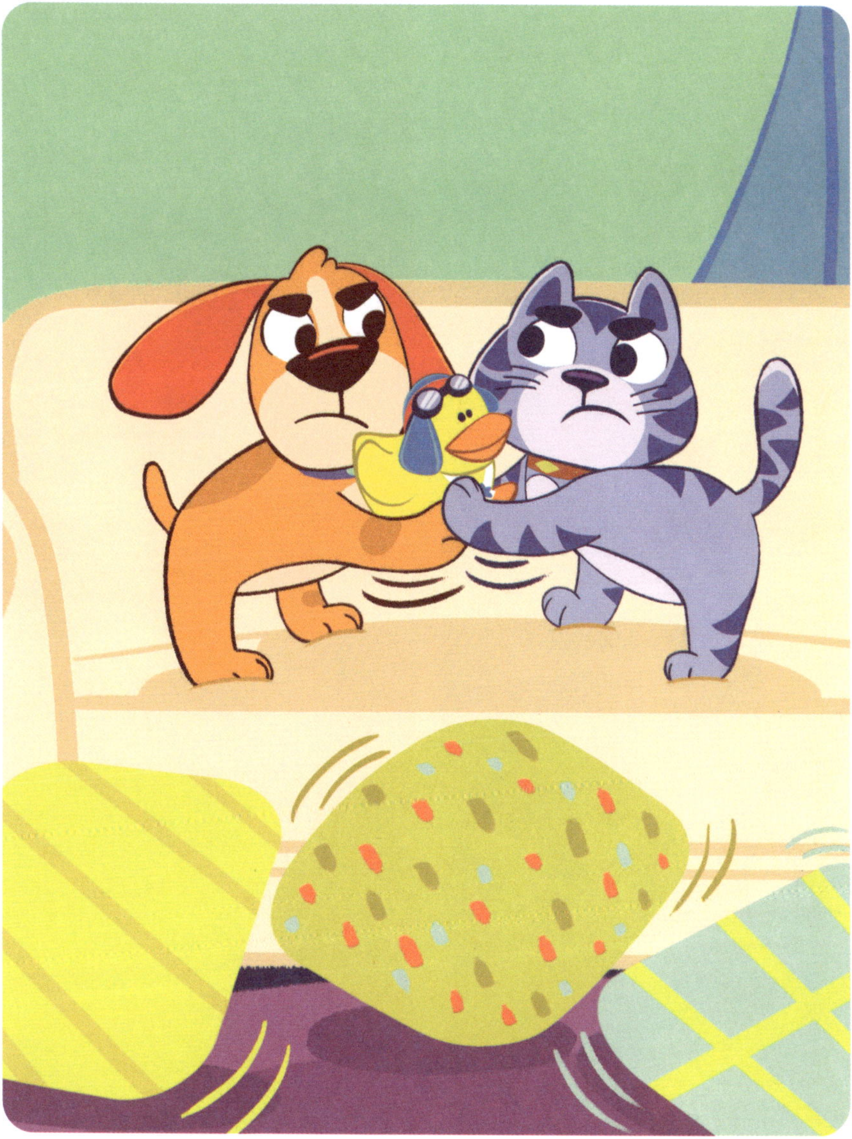

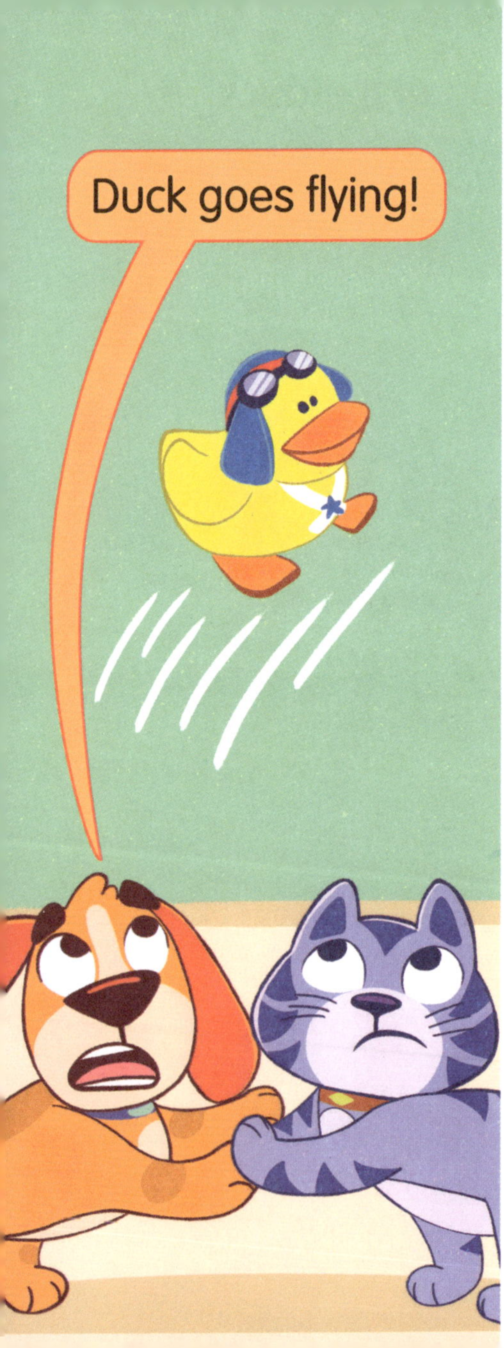
Duck goes flying!
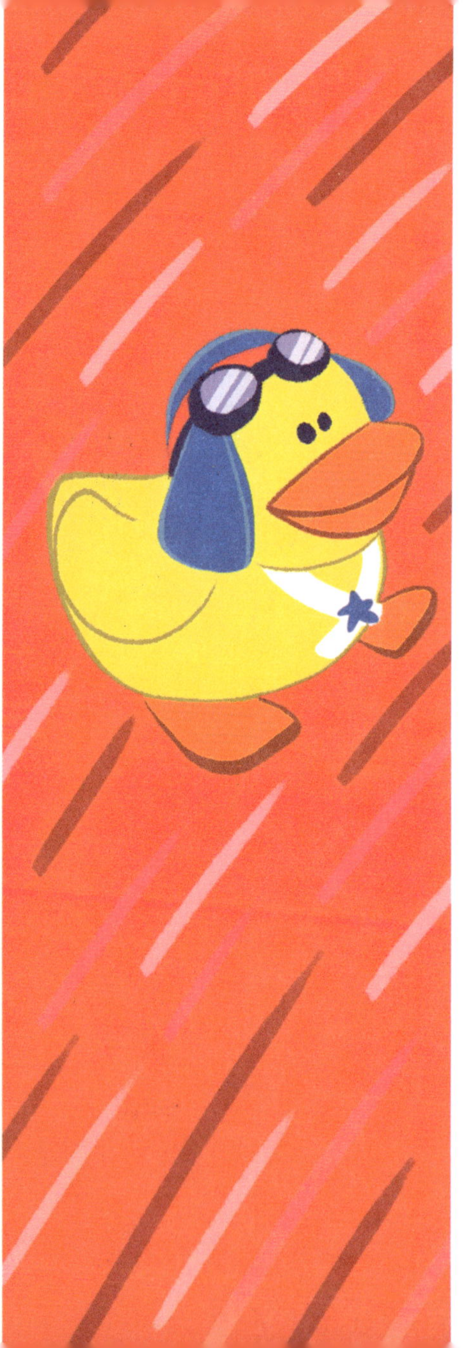

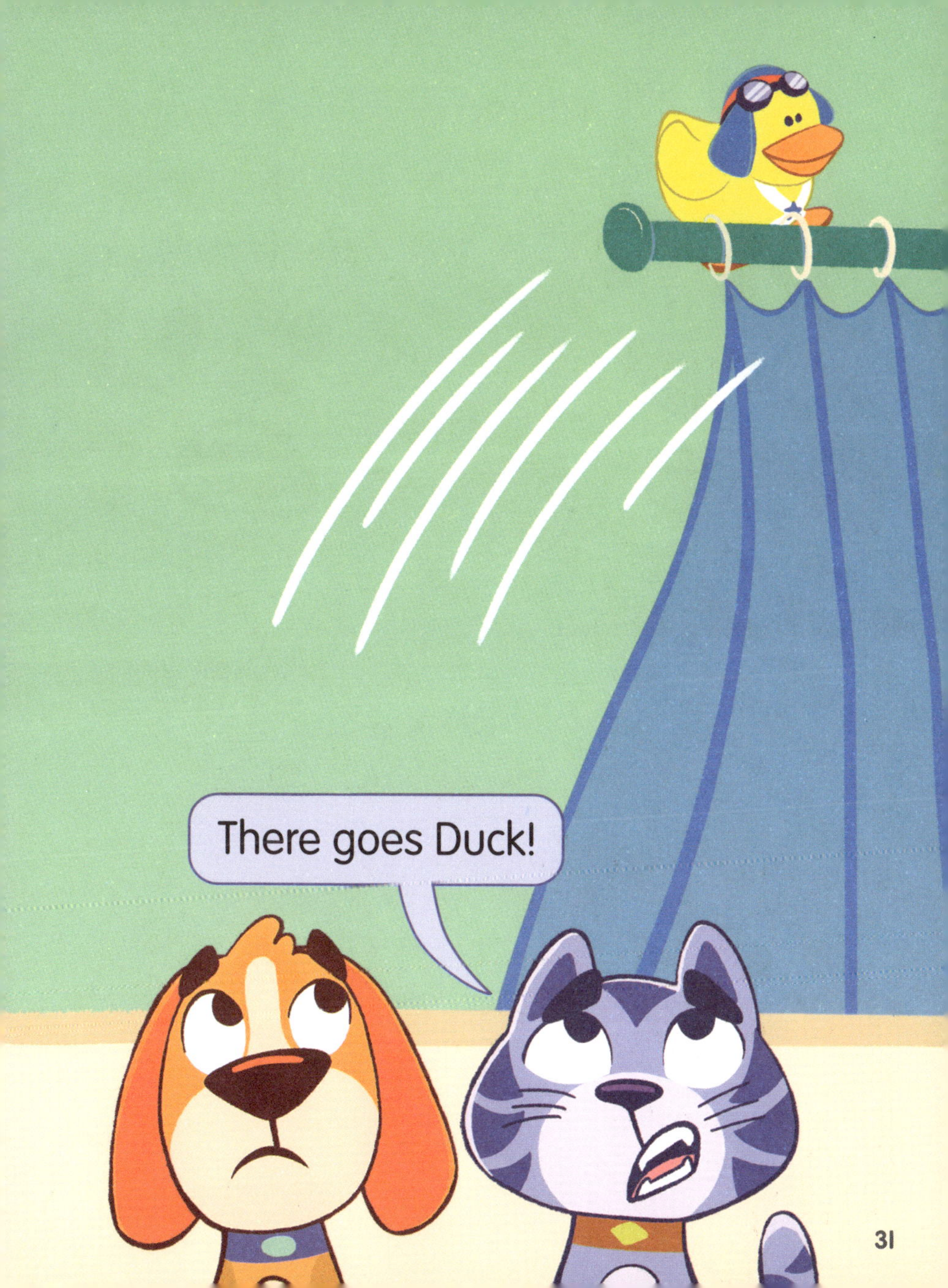
There goes Duck!

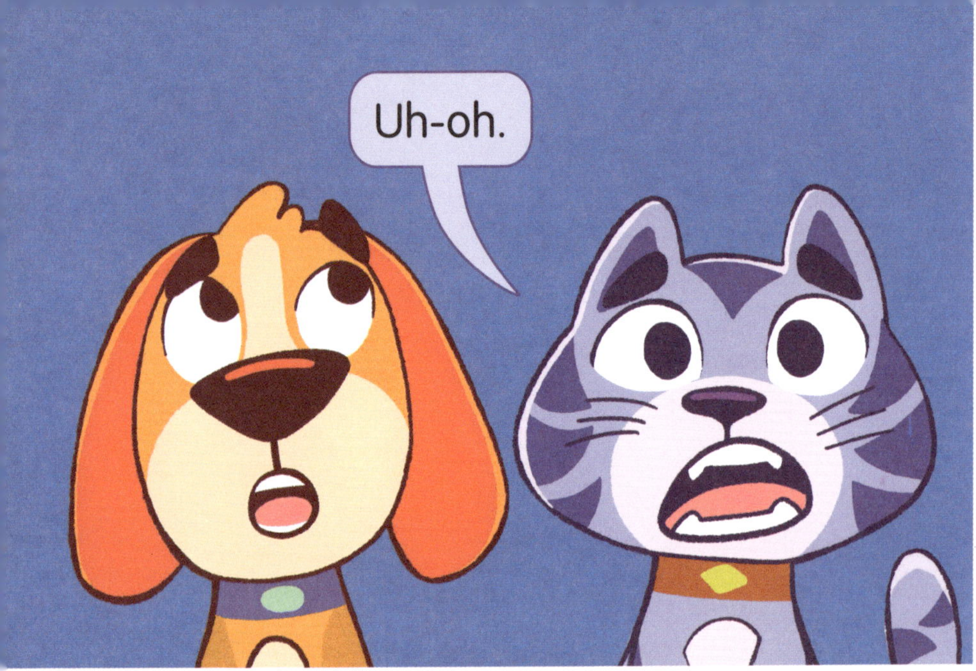
Uh-oh.

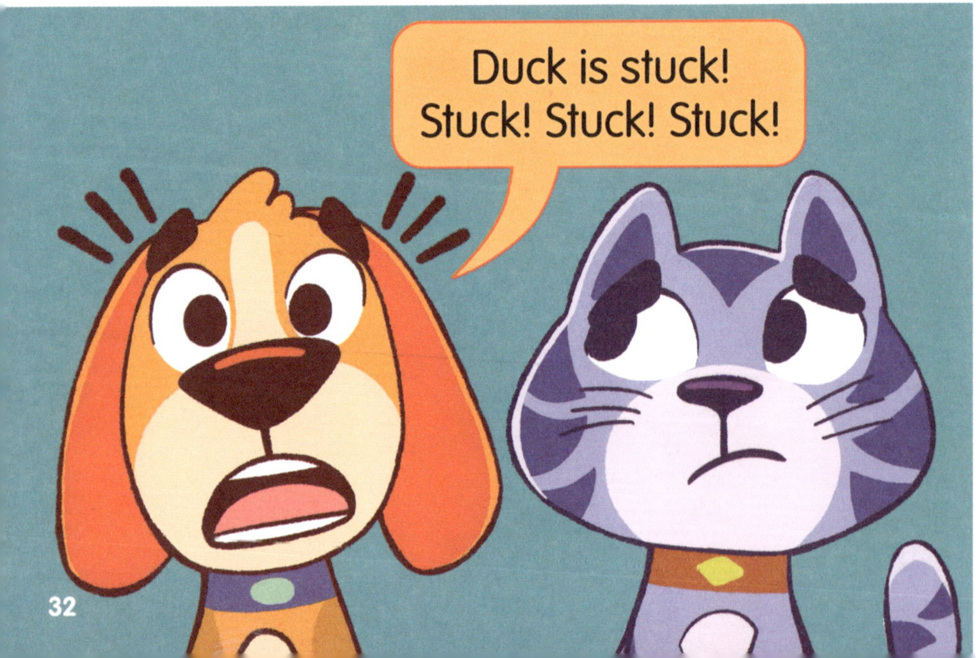
Duck is stuck!
Stuck! Stuck! Stuck!

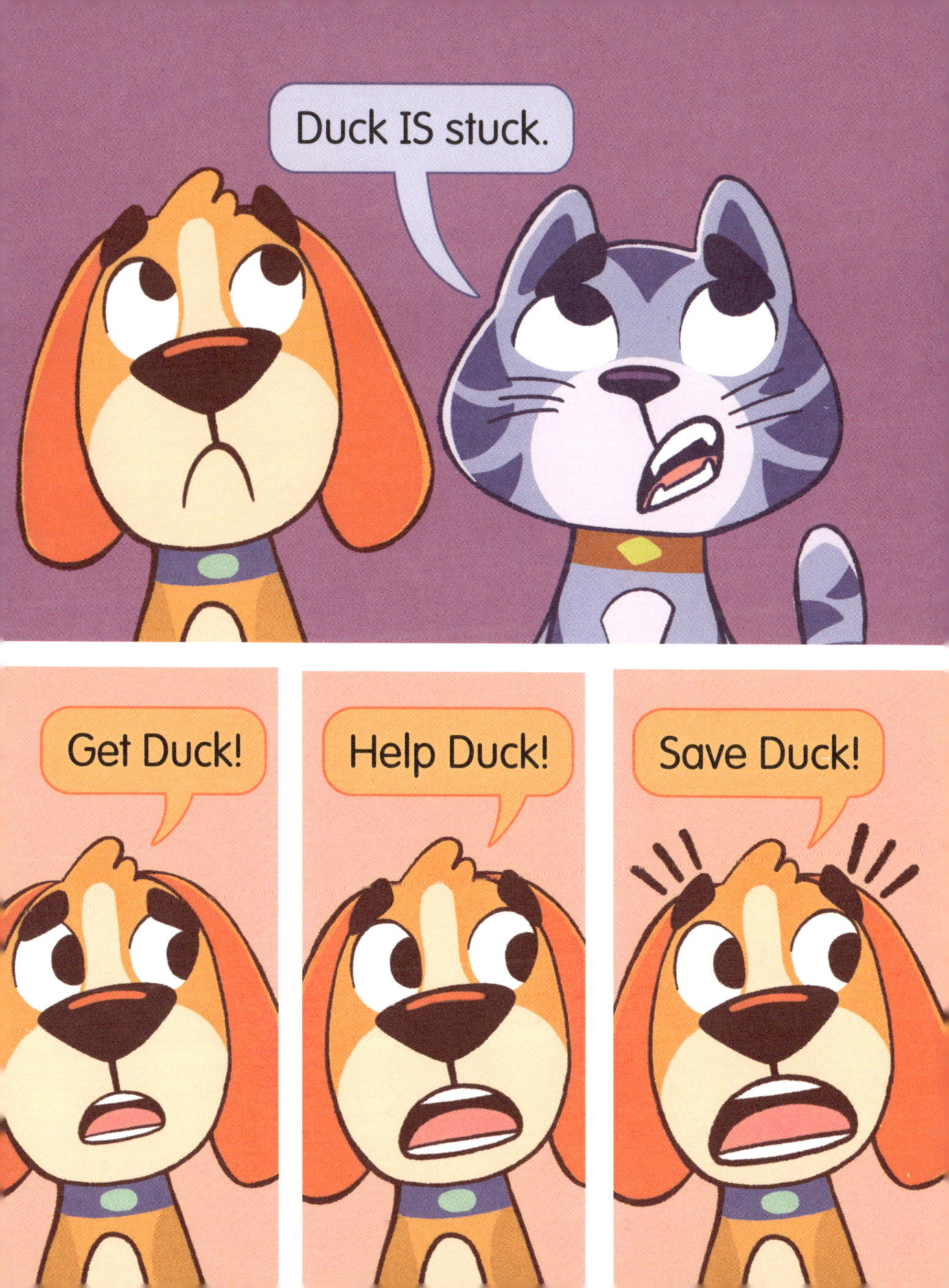
Duck IS stuck.
Get Duck!
Help Duck!
Save Duck!

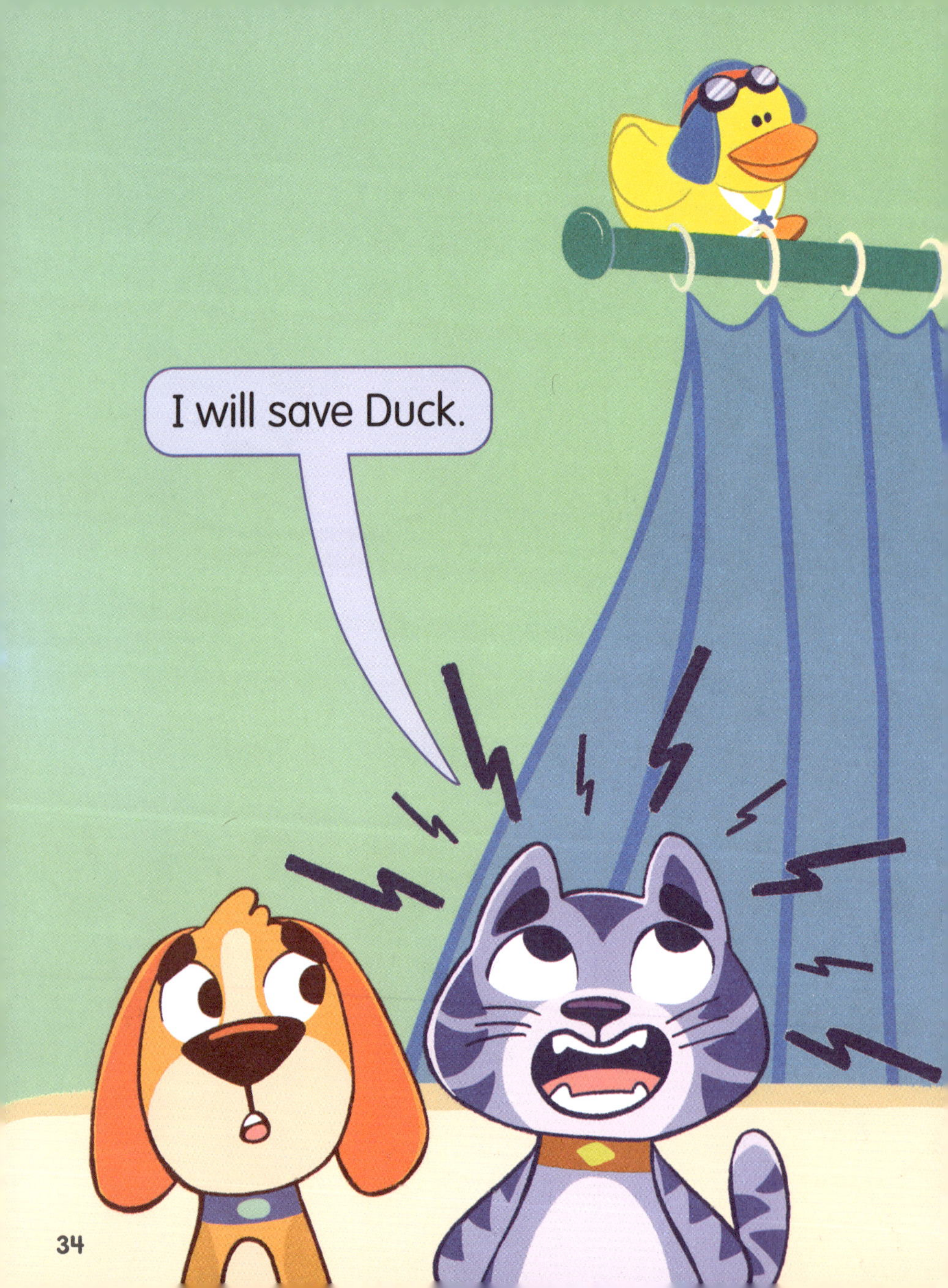
I will save Duck.

Scratch goes up.

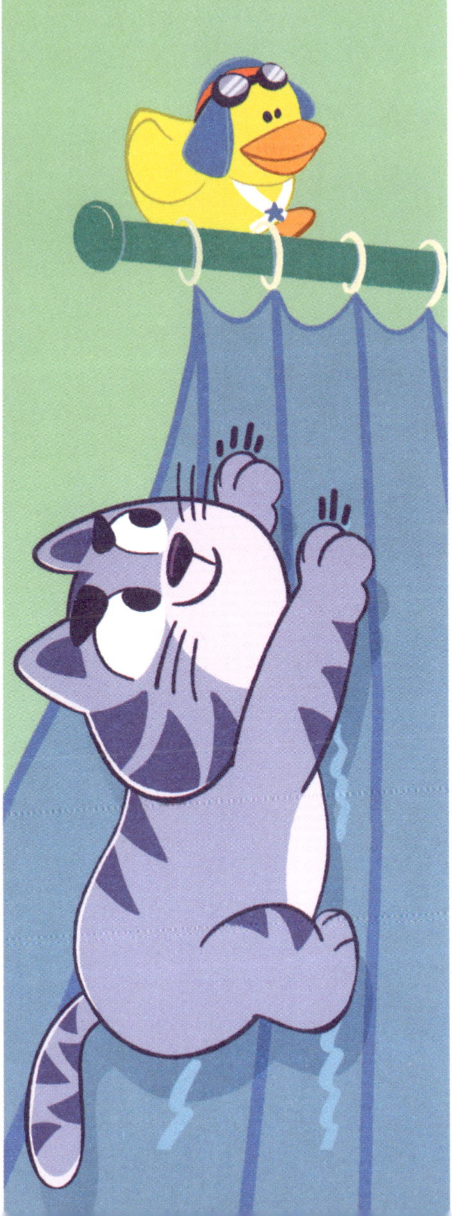

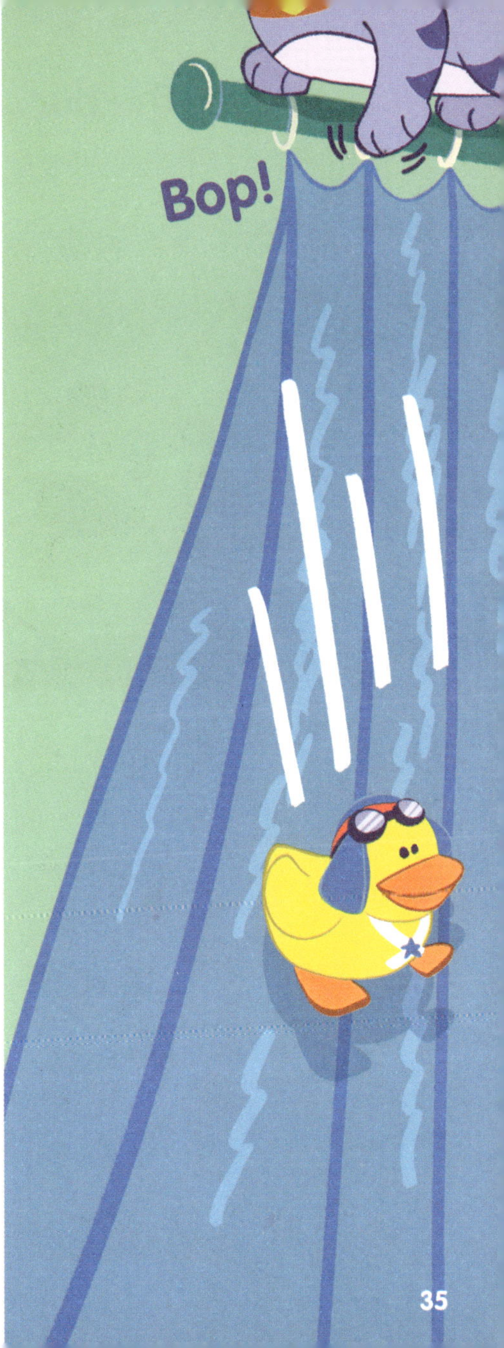
Bop!

The duck goes down.

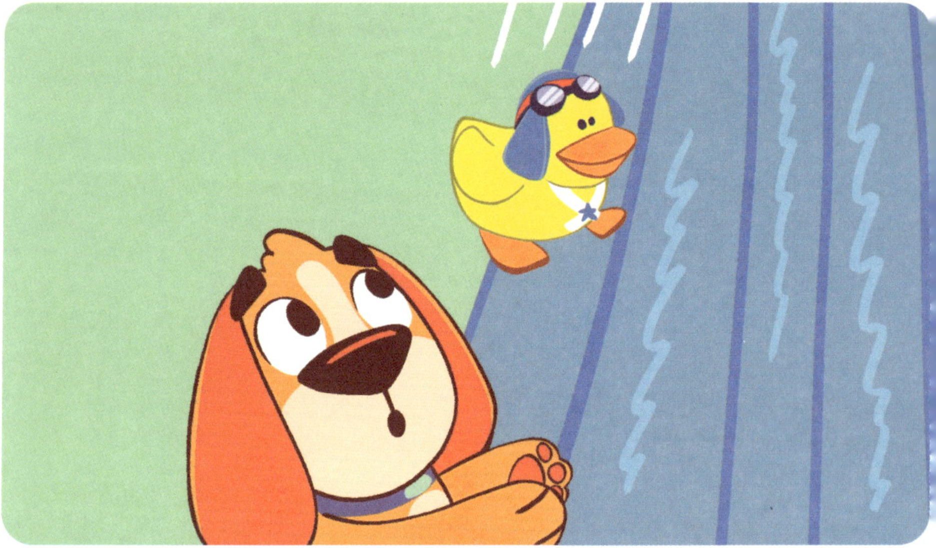

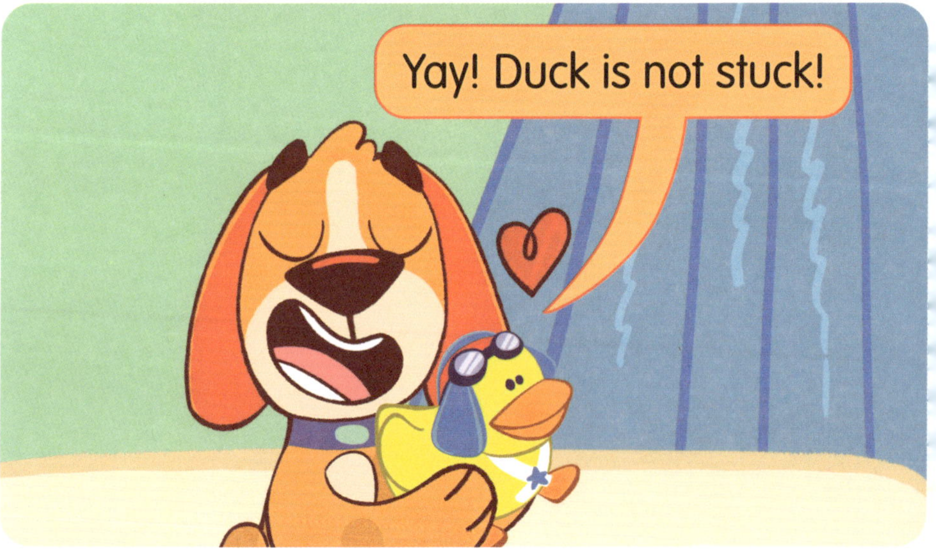
Yay! Duck is not stuck!

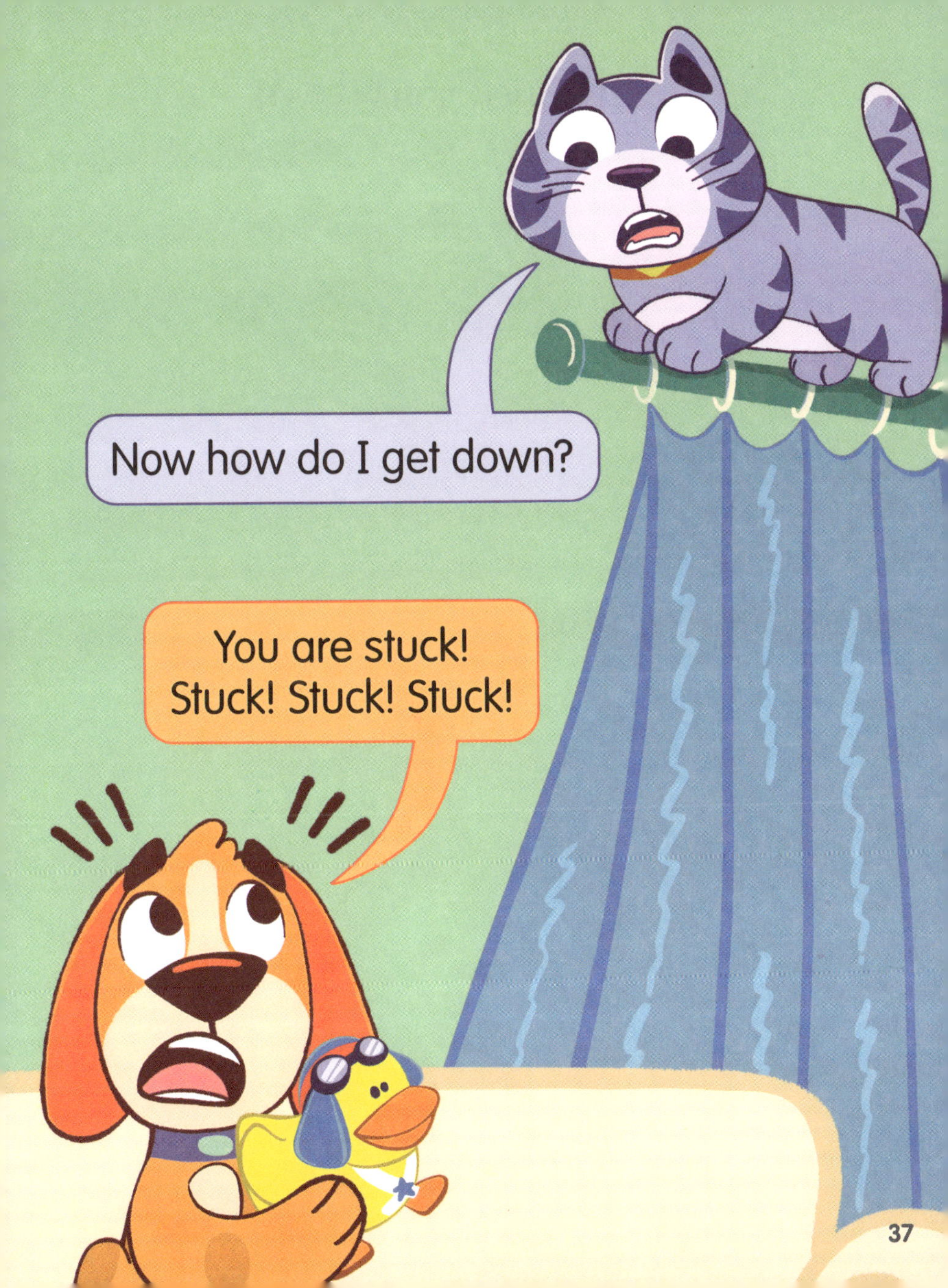
Now how do I get down?
You are stuck!
Stuck! Stuck! Stuck!

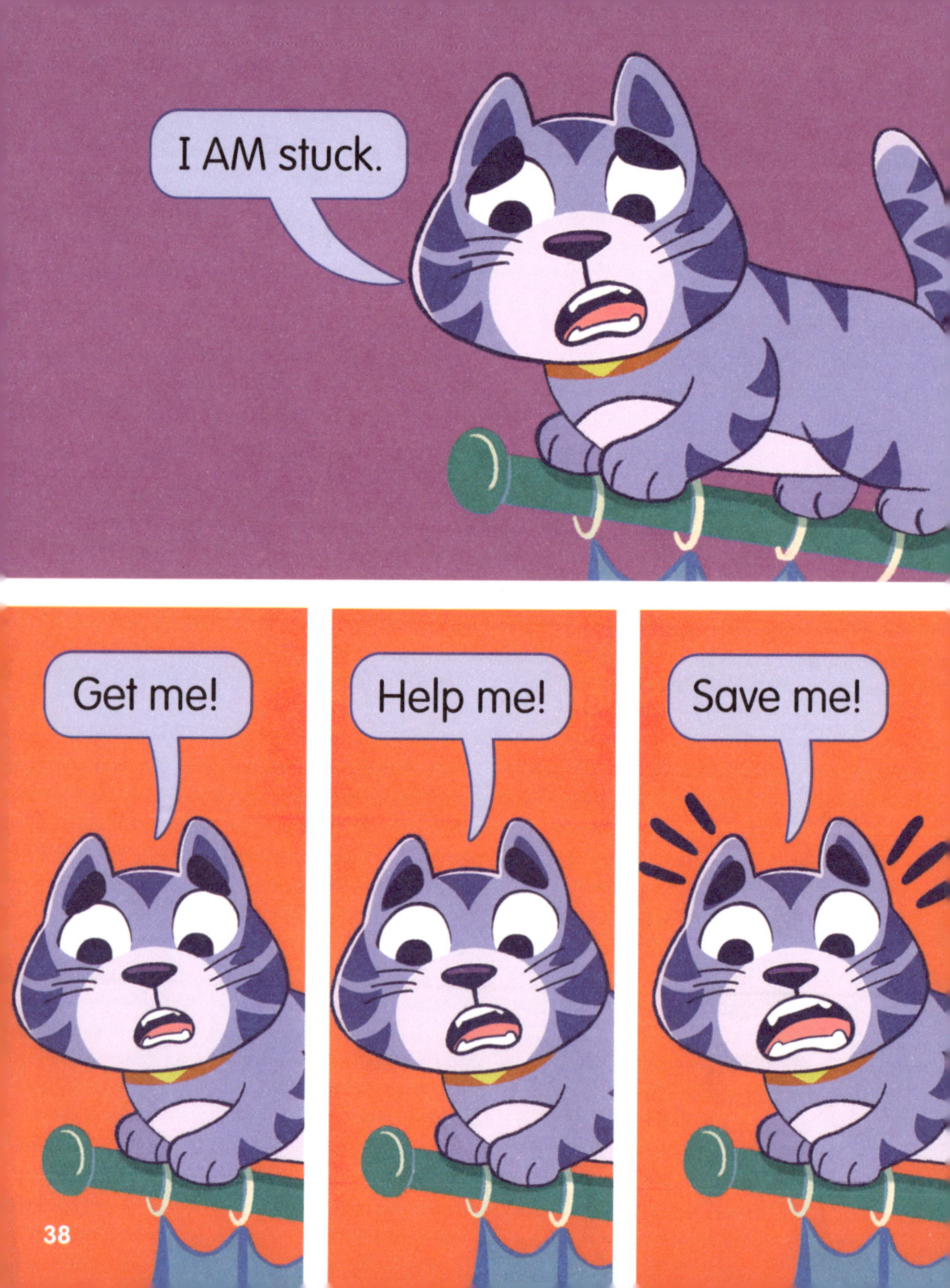
I AM stuck.
Get me!
Help me!
Save me!

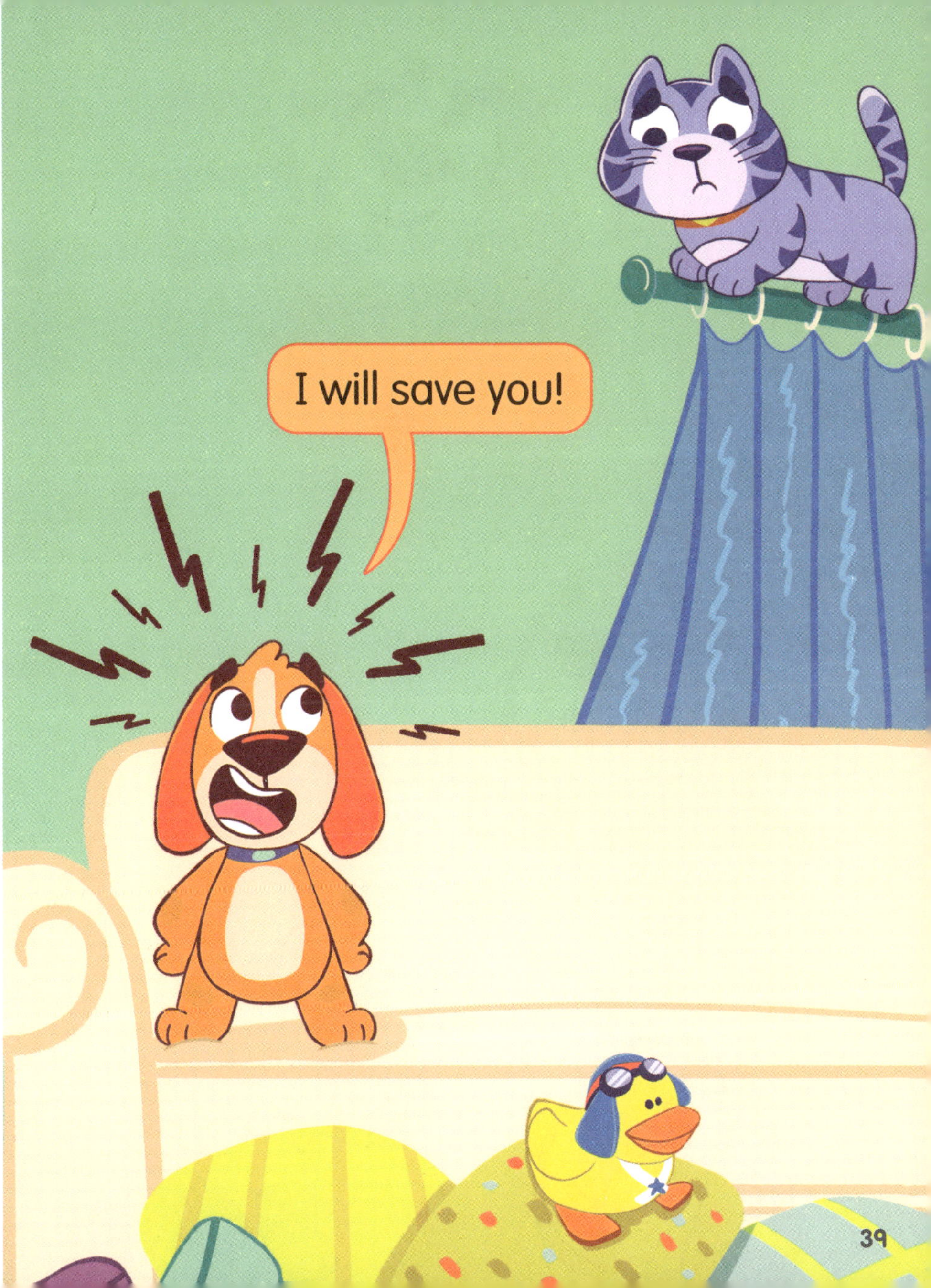
I will save you!

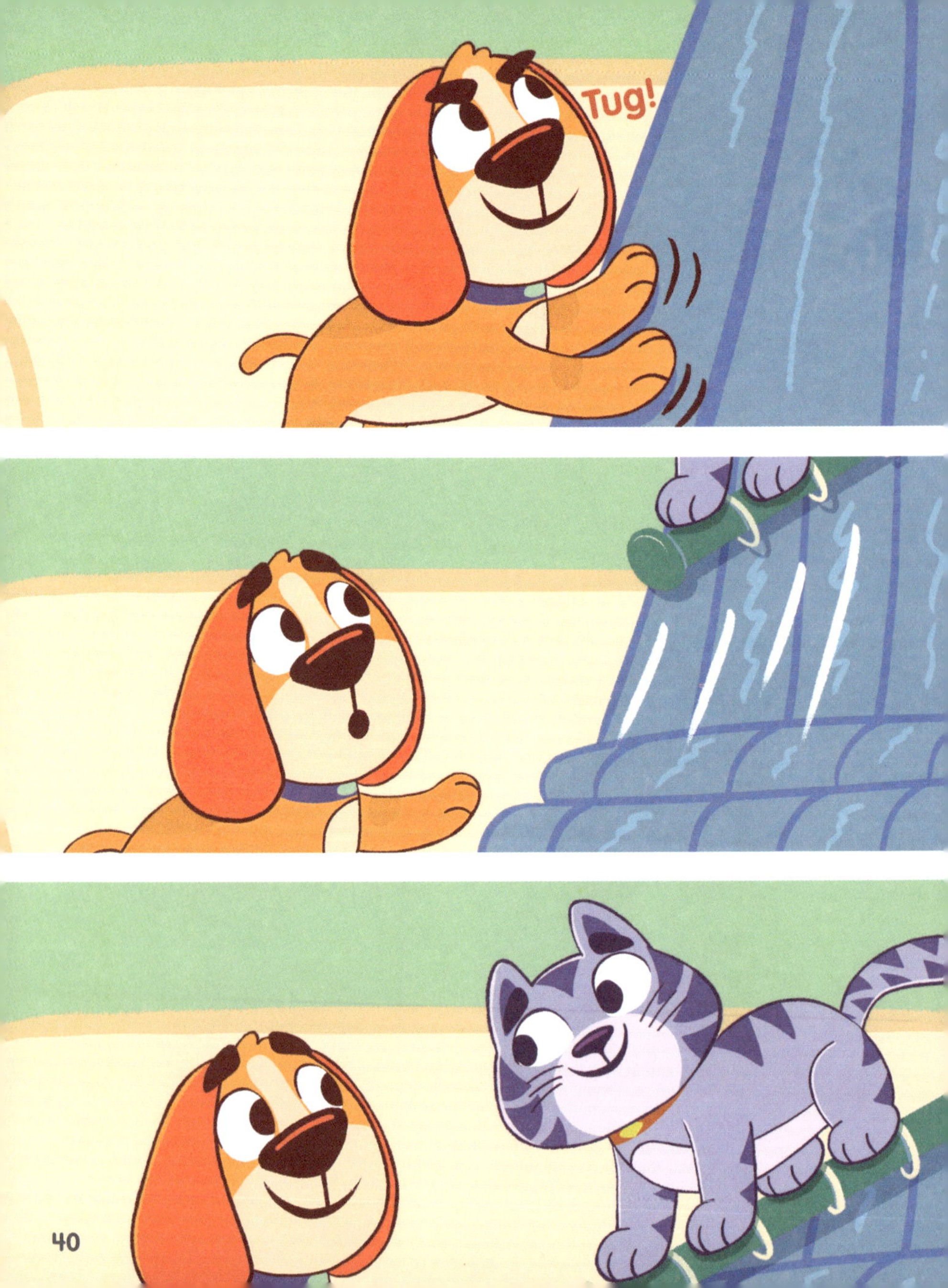
Tug!

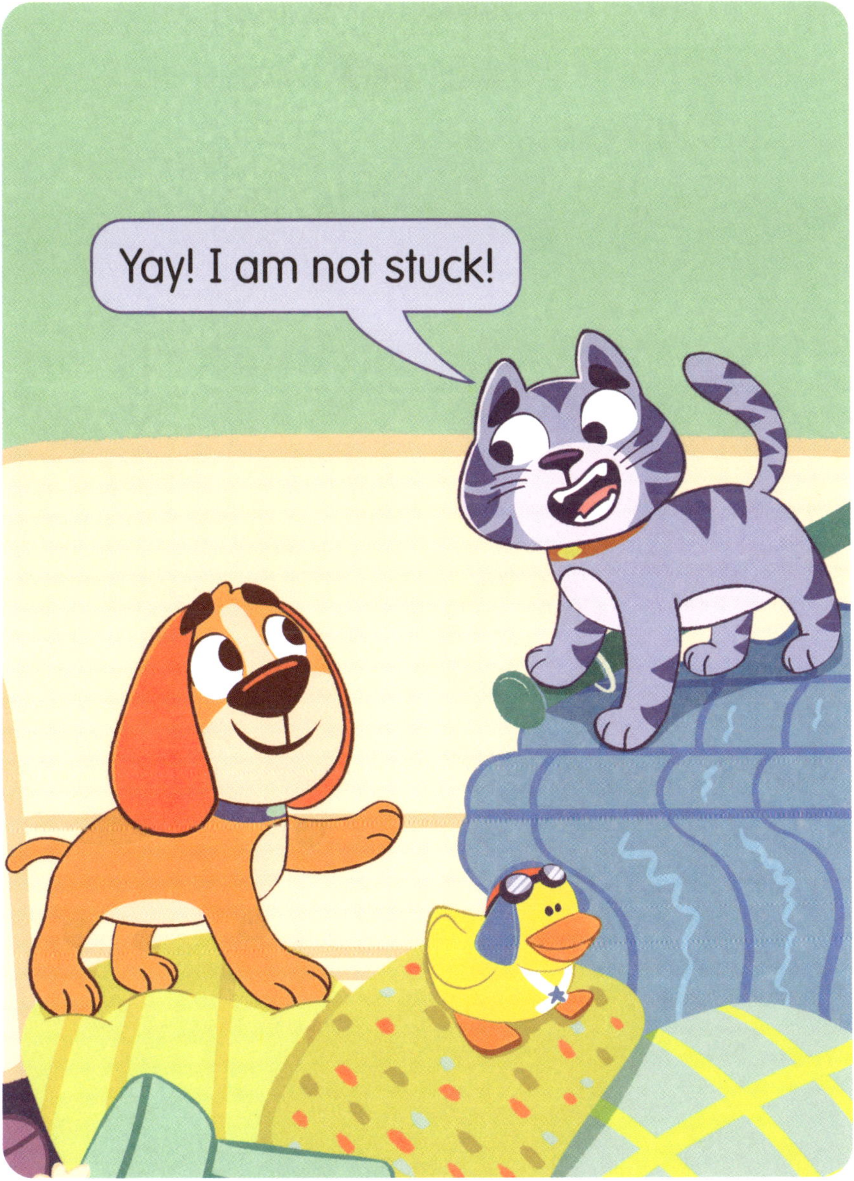
Yay! I am not stuck!

Sniff and Scratch are happy.

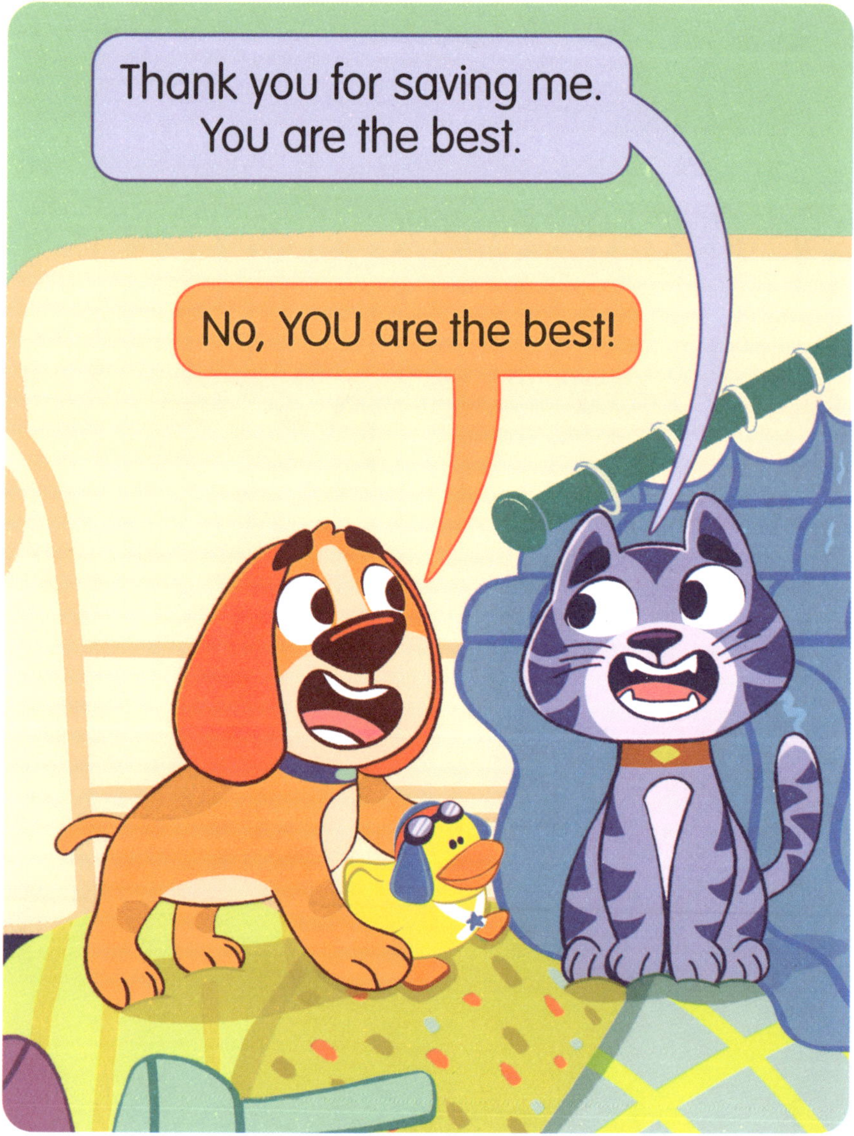
Thank you for saving me. You are the best.
No, YOU are the best!

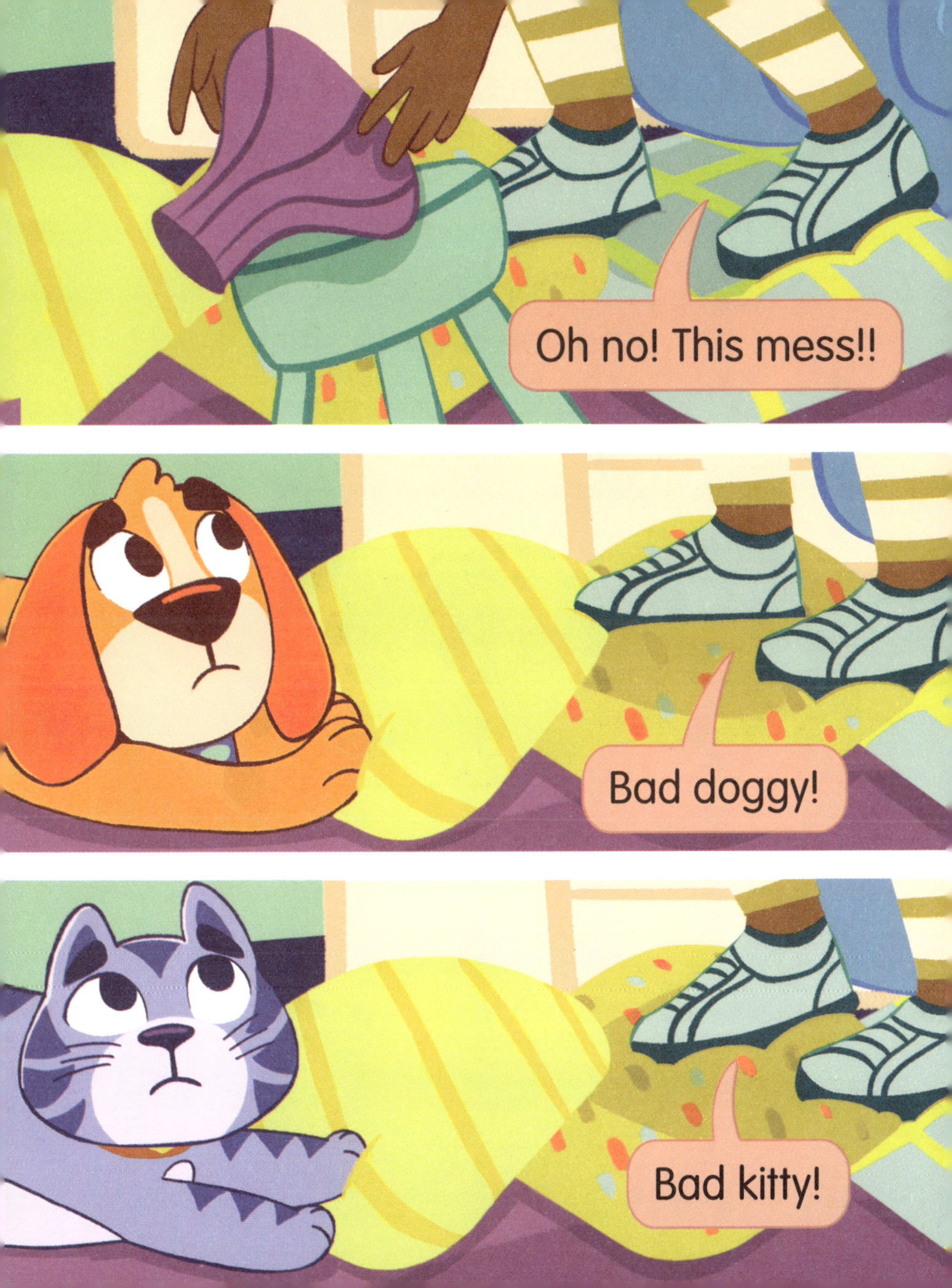
Oh no! This mess!!
Bad doggy!
Bad kitty!

Sniff and Scratch are still happy.

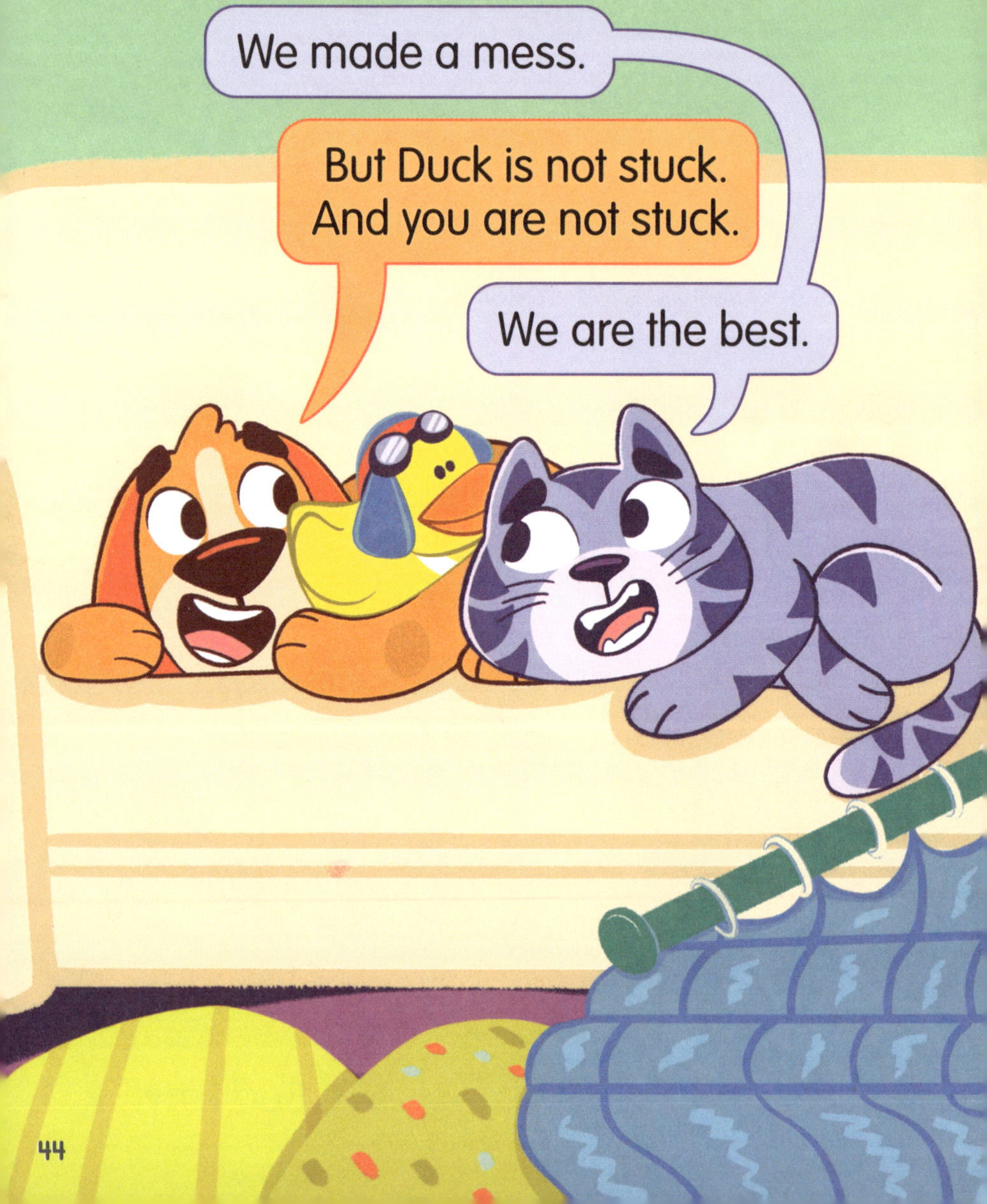
We made a mess.
But Duck is not stuck. And you are not stuck.
We are the best.

About the Creators

Vicky Fang lives in Mountain View, California, with her husband, their two sons, a few sea monkeys, and one pet rhinoceros beetle. They are now considering what their next new pet might be. She is also the author of the Scholastic Branches early chapter book series Layla and the Bots.

Luisa Leal is originally from Venezuela, but she now calls Nevada home, where she designs characters and backgrounds for games. Telling stories through pictures has always been her passion, and illustrating a picture book is a dream come true for her. When she's not designing, you can find her swimming, riding her bike, or planning her next adventure!

YOU CAN DRAW DUCK!

1. Draw Duck's body. The angles are all C shapes. Give Duck two dot eyes.

2. Add a beak and goggles.

3. Draw one wing on Duck's side. Give Duck two feet.

4. Draw Duck's pilot hat. It has a stripe and two ear flaps.

5. Add Duck's pilot scarf. Draw a small star where it overlaps itself.

6. Color in your drawing!

WHAT'S YOUR STORY?

Sniff loves Duck. Scratch wants a toy, too. Imagine **you** give a new toy to Scratch. What would it look like? Would Scratch love it? Write and draw your story!

scholastic.com/acorn